ECHOLOCATION

a novel

Engine Books
PO Box 44167
Indianapolis, IN 46244
enginebooks.org

Also available in paperback, audio book, and eBook from Engine Books.

Photos featuring the landscapes of *Echolocation* by Myfanwy Collins.

Printed in the United States of America

10   9   8   7   6   5   4   3   2   1

ISBN: 978-0-9835477-9-2

Library of Congress Control Number: 2011939928

ECHOLOCATION

a novel

Myfanwy Collins

*To the Chateaugay Memorial library,
I love this town.
Thank you for feeding me
in my youth.*

Engine Books
Indianapolis

I dedicate this book to Allen and Henry,
the two brightest stars in my sky

WHEN THE SLIP OF SAW through trunk was buttery, liquid, and verging on gentle, Geneva was moved to tears. Her body felt as though it were cutting through the tree: the rings, the history of droughts and hailstorms, the sap that could have been her own blood, dripping, weeping at her feet. It felt like a betrayal, this taking of saw to tree. But Clint was out of work again. They needed money.

She was down by the quarry, just off the old logging road, claiming a patch of ground Auntie Marie had given her for a wedding present—her dowry. "Don't tell him, though," Marie suggested about the wooded acre. "Keep that land to yourself." Geneva had thought of using the trees for sugaring as Auntie Marie had proposed but now it was too late. She was taking the trees for cheap firewood to sell to tourists at a roadside stand. Such a waste.

The tinny song of the wood thrush carried above other birds' calls. Eerie and mechanical, it was her favorite birdsong. As if her fractured heart called out into the world. She paused before moving on to the next tree. Listened above the idle of her saw while the song intensified, grew frantic. Warning? Was it warning her? No. The thrush was singing as it always had done and always would do.

But she felt off that morning, a blue shakiness she couldn't otherwise explain. It didn't have anything to do with the fact that Clint hadn't come home the night before or that their electric bill was overdue. It was something else, something blurry around the edges. When she looked back on this day later all she would think was, "I should have known."

She left her dog, Mr. Pink, behind that day because he'd gone gimpy in his left hind leg, and she thought maybe her bad feeling was about him. Another mistake, she would later realize. Her bad feeling had nothing to do with Mr. Pink, curled up on an old afghan by the woodstove. His leg was bad, and he didn't have much more time to live, but he would not die that day. He would spend his day warm and comfortable, waiting for his next meal.

As always she checked the gauge of her old truck before she left home, noting that she had enough gas to drive to the trees and back. This was her biggest mistake. She would need that gas and then some. A full tank of gas would have made things turn out entirely different. Entirely.

It was adrenaline that saved Geneva. And pressure from the tourniquet she tied around her upper arm, using her belt, her one good hand, and her teeth. After the saw kicked back and cut through the flesh of her left forearm, she sensed more than knew that she needed to move—that she needed to ignore the white lights flickering around her eyes, and ignore, especially, the pain, the gushing blood. She needed to move. So that's what she'd done. Tied the tourniquet and run to the truck, hopped in it, and drove toward town, toward help. When the truck ran out of gas partway there, she didn't sit and wait for someone to notice. She got out of that truck and she ran like hell down the road, trailing pools and splatters of blood. She remembered thinking that the blood was an odd color on the pavement—iridescent, like the tail of a My Little Pony. She marveled at her own blood as she ran. The leprechaun color of it, granting wishes.

Terry Plunker saw her first and loaded her on his ATV in search of help. It took some doing, though. By that time she was in shock and babbling about the miracle of her blood. "It will save you," she said. "I have seen the truth in it."

He knew women like this. He knew their kind, which was why Plunker was gentle and eased her into getting on the ATV. "Set still now," he said as he moved the vehicle forward. "You set still."

"Looked like a goddamned horror movie," is what he said after they got her safely to the clinic. "Like that *Carrie* on the night of the prom. So much frickin' blood." So much blood, in fact, Plunker nearly passed out himself at the sight of her. "Her arm was cut clean off," he said. "Clean off." He sounded almost impressed. Like he didn't know a man alive who could have survived what she had. Almost like he believed her arm would grow right back out of that stump.

Regardless of everyone's best intentions, though, most of the arm could not be saved. And so beautiful Geneva would henceforth be known as one-armed Geneva—still beautiful, but flawed. Clint felt so bad about his wife's disfigurement and how, had he been a better man, he might have prevented it, that he went down the street to the funeral home, met with the undertaker, and picked out a top of the line casket—white, silver-handled, with pink silk interior.

There was no viewing but there was a small service at the graveyard, led by Father O'Connor. Geneva was there, dressed in black, mourning, and as they lowered the baby-sized casket that encased what was once her living arm, complete with the engagement ring and wedding band still on the finger, into the ground, Geneva dropped a shovelful of dirt on it, looked right at Clint, and said,

"Ashes to ashes and dust to dust." Later she vowed those would be the last words she ever said to him. Ever.

2

CHERI ROUNDED THE FINAL CORNER at the coffee shop and noted that the light cast on the brick apartment buildings recalled the light on the brick wall behind the bowling alley when she was a kid. Back where she and Geneva would hang to smoke a joint and drink some beers before going to the school gym for roller-skating on a Friday night. The sight of it made her want to wing around and around, weaving in and out of the lines on the basketball court. She and Geneva, cracking the whip, laughing so hard they thought they would pee.

Now it was the end of another day in a string of days, of days, of days. The only way she could measure time anymore was by what month *Spin* magazine she happened to be reading and even that was not a good indicator. It might have arrived early or it might be an old issue. Time was dusty. Time was irrelevant.

But the next day Cheri would head north, back home, to say goodbye to her Auntie Marie, who might have longer to live had she not refused treatment. "I'm waiting for a miracle," is how Auntie Marie put it on the phone. But there had been no miracle, and according to the doctor, her aunt would die within the week.

Cheri was going back home, a border town in upstate New York, seven miles from Canada. A little patch of nothing made up of dairy farms in the valleys and boarded up iron ore mines in the mountains; a town of old folks waiting to die and young people dying to leave. Auntie Marie owned a store-cum-gas station a breath away from the border crossing. It was a first stop for Canadians coming down to cottage at the lake and the last stop for Americans on their way to Montreal to score some hash.

She knew she should have gone sooner. Spent more time. Said a proper goodbye. Tended to her roots. Auntie Marie always said, "Don't forget your roots, girl." Roots were nothing to Cheri. They could be torn up and thrown in the trash, left behind. Roots held you back and she'd already broken free of them. Still, her life was supposed to have turned out differently. She wasn't supposed to be working in a used record store. She wasn't supposed to be sleeping with strung-out boys in garage bands. She shouldn't have been spending her nights out at clubs, smoking, getting wasted.

Her bones ached and she felt like she might be losing her hearing. She had lately believed the skin near her ears was sagging and that there were wrinkles in her neck and, horribly, at the edge of her jaw where her ears met her face. She was tired and ready to have someone take care of her or to have what was coming to her, some money that she could use to go away someplace quiet and think. There was something else bugging her, too, but she couldn't quite put her finger on it, or more characteristically, was ignoring it, pushing it down, avoiding it, though what was bugging her felt very much like home.

It had been almost four years since Cheri was last home. Four years since Geneva married Clint, and since Cheri said, "He's a pig." Those were the words she'd used and after that there was not much else to say, especially because Geneva would hear none of it. Geneva's disregard proved fortuitous, though, for it gave Cheri the nudge she needed, and in some ways had always hoped for. Once she was done standing up on the altar next to Geneva and Clint as they said their vows, she'd left town, eighteen years old then and on her own. She didn't even flinch when Auntie Marie first called and told her of her illness. Not until Geneva herself called and said, "Come home now. It's time," did she flinch.

Cheri forgot what her own face looked like in the bathroom mirror back there under the ticking fluorescent tube and stark-white northern sky. Had her face been soft then? Had it been open?

She was not soft now. She was blunt: hair cut to match the army of kids, the friends she hung out with. Black fingernail polish and clunky shoes. She would look neither pretty nor hopeful in her auntie's pink-tiled bathroom. She was quite sure of that. But what tugged at her was that maybe a visit to the safety and simplicity of home would erase some of the crap that was her life and bring her back to an understanding of the person she was and what she wanted.

It had to.

The light on the tenements caught her eye again and for a second she felt someone's hand grab hers in crack the whip. She felt the thrill of speeding forward and of letting go.

CHERI OPENED THE DOOR to the typical jingling of the bell. The sound that was safety and home, that was you are here and you cannot leave. And the smell of the store: Nilla Wafers softening in their boxes, Vicks Vapo-rub, stale beer. Geneva stood behind the counter, half obscured by the enormous antique cash register Auntie Marie couldn't bear to part with even though they never used it anymore, its keys long before having stuck in place. Geneva looked up and

Cheri felt a zip of tinfoil thread through her gut, cutting away all silvery and cool. Geneva was still as beautiful as she had been the last time Cheri saw her. She had been one of those long-limbed girls men looked at in that needful way long before she reached puberty. Auntie Marie had always been careful of Geneva, kept her covered up, hidden away, though she seemed almost proud of the child's beauty and even more so when the beautiful child turned into an even more beautiful woman.

Not so with Cheri.

"Welcome home," Geneva said.

"Thanks." Cheri let her bag slip off her shoulder to the floor. She wanted to say more but there was too much space between them and Cheri could not figure out what words of hers might close that gap.

"She's waiting on you." Geneva nodded toward the side door that led to the house. Cheri picked up her bag and walked across the floor. As she passed the register, she turned to say something, a "Sorry for taking so long to get here," or "I've been busy and couldn't make it sooner," but she gawked instead because it was then she noticed that the place where Geneva's left arm had been was now an empty sleeve, pinned up at the shoulder. Geneva caught Cheri's eye and turned her back to stock the cigarette display.

Cheri stood for a moment and puzzled over what to say—how to ask about the arm—but could find nothing suitable. Instead, she ducked her head and made her way quickly into the house. It was quiet but for the sound of a television toward the back where Auntie Marie's bedroom was. She followed the frantic wail of a game show.

The door to her aunt's bedroom was ajar. Cheri nudged it with her foot. Auntie Marie was on her back, asleep, mouth open, slack-jawed, hands clasped across her chest. Cheri took a step back to let her sleep, and Auntie Marie sat up with a start, opened her eyes and her mouth and let out a yelp. "Who is it?" she called out, her hand scrabbling along amongst the brown bottles on the nightstand for her glasses. There was a sound, a jangle, which Cheri later realized was the intravenous morphine drip on a wheeled pole next to the bed.

"It's just me, Auntie," she said.

Auntie Marie found her glasses, put them on, and squinted through the smudged lenses. "Get over here and give an old woman a hug," she said, holding her arms out for Cheri. "I thought you were your mother standing there." Cheri bent for the hug. Beneath her hands she could feel the knobby bones of her aunt's spine. It was the map of a dying body, one caving in on itself, turning back to dust.

IN THE FAMILIAR KITCHEN, cabinets sanded down and painted glossy white every other year, fresh gingham curtains in the window, Cheri prepared to cut a sandwich straight through the middle. A vertical cut. Her aunt shuffled into the room, half pulling, half leaning on her morphine pole as Cheri started to lower the knife.

"You forget everything I taught you?" Auntie Marie grabbed the knife away and demonstrated the proper diagonal. "Like this," she said. Butter oozed out the side of the sandwich and she swiped it with the knife and buttered the next slice of bread.

"Let me," Cheri said, reaching for the knife. "You should sit." Though she spoke with her typical unflagging animation, no more was Marie the large-bosomed, rosy-cheeked woman who took Cheri onto her lap and kept her close when her mother took off down to Florida with her new boyfriend years and years before. "She thought it would be best if you stayed here with me for the rest of the year, Cheri," Marie had said to her when she was seven. "This way you can finish up school with your friends, with Geneva." A foster child who had never gone back to her parents, Geneva filled the roles of daughter/sister/cousin in their family.

It seemed logical for Cheri to stay, but when her mother never came back for her and when no one ever mentioned it again she eventually realized that she was living with Auntie Marie for good. And it was okay, only seeing her mother once or twice a year when she visited, until even those visits drifted off into nothing.

Now they sat across from each other at the table. "Glad to have you home," Auntie Marie said matter-of-factly and took a dainty bite of her sandwich. Cheri could tell her aunt meant it, that she was glad to have her home. And Cheri was glad, too, and also filled with desperation—to escape, to flee.

"Thought Geneva was off living in the woods with that Clint," Cheri said to change the subject.

"I needed helping out. She needed work. So, here she is." Auntie Marie shrugged, put her sandwich down and took a deep, wincing breath.

"What happened?" Cheri said and caught her aunt's glance toward the door.

"Chainsaw," Auntie Marie said. Cheri nodded, watched as she swallowed the bit of sandwich she was chewing, the food nearly visible as it made its way down the thin throat. "Got her to wise up and leave that jackass of a husband, always heading over the border, down to the nudie bars." Auntie Marie pushed her plate away. Shook her head in disgust. "That's enough for me," she said, stifling a burp. "Go out and take a walk. Go feed them cats or something."

"You sure?" Cheri felt closed up in the house, the darkness of the rooms pushing on her. She was desperate to be outside, to catch the sweet mournful call of the white-throated sparrow lifting across the field.

"Go," Auntie Marie said as she pumped more morphine into her system.

———

THE CATS NEVER CAME IN the house, never were petted. They lived in and around an old shed out back. Auntie Marie fed them and named them, but when they became too plentiful she would shoot some of them with her rifle or drown their kittens in the stream. "It's the humane thing to do," her auntie claimed, and wouldn't listen to Geneva that there were studies that said otherwise. That killing them made them breed more frequently to make up for their losses.

Cheri hated the cats. When she was younger she would try to tame some kitten or other and always ended up with sorry red welts on her hands and arms. Once a scratch on her neck became infected and she got a fever and was hospitalized. The scar still remained, like a puffy boil. She touched it then as she poured Agway dry cat food into four large metal basins.

Cats slunk from under the back porch and out of the bushes at the sound of the pellets hitting the tin. A few of them wound their bodies around her calves but she remained unmoved.

The field was golden stalks of long-past-summer grass, dead and waiting for snow. Rust colored milkweed leaves dotted the landscape here and there along with bright red chokecherries. A line of denuded sugar maples and firs circled the land, leading to a darkening woods. Cheri took off for the edge of the trees. She looked back once and saw her auntie's head framed in the window, illuminated by television light. Her head listed to one side, asleep? Dead? It was unclear. Auntie Marie gave the impression of one who was no longer of this earth. She was at that moment as fleeting as a feral cat.

————

GENEVA WALKED THE CREAKING FLOORS of her room and talked to her lost arm. Every night she told the arm what it meant to her, how it helped her live the life she had lived all these years. How bereft she was without it. More than anything else that had gone missing in her life—her parents, Cheri, Clint, and Mr. Pink, who died in his sleep shortly after she came home from the hospital—she missed this limb.

She set up votive candles on her dresser surrounding a photo of her younger self wearing a strapless dress. It was from her prom. She and Clint had gone together but now she'd cut him out of the photo and left only herself and her two arms—beautiful, symmetrical. Each time she passed the small shrine, she nodded and said, "Please come back." Some nights she felt a tingling where the arm had been, felt the fingers on her left hand opening and closing, grasping out for a connection with the rest of her flesh.

But this night she felt nothing. No matter how much she willed it, the arm would not feel. Cheri had come back and was taking away all of the energy that Geneva had so carefully channeled. Cheri was the dark and brooding type that people worried over, the type who sucked all of the energy out of the room, leaving nothing behind for those who might really need it. Leaving nothing behind, but always leaving.

CHERI FOUND THE SPOT in the woods, a little clearing surrounded by hemlock and firs, where she and Geneva would go when they were younger. At first it was the place they set up as a house, where one of them would take turns playing the father and the other the mother. More often than not, Geneva ended up being the mother because Cheri grew tired of taking care of the babies and feeding her deadbeat husband.

When they were older, this was one of the secret places where they brought their pilfered beer and cigarettes. Sometimes they built a small fire and stayed out past dark, lying on their backs, fighting with each other over who could count the most shooting stars, faking it sometimes and making wishes anyway. "I wish we could stay like this forever," Geneva often said and Cheri nodded and agreed. And even though part of her wanted to be near Geneva always and forever, in her mind she was traveling as far away from the spot in the woods, the store, her aunt, her best friend, as she could. She wanted to follow the path of her mother, but not so that she would find her; instead, she wanted to know what it felt like to be the one leaving, instead of the one left behind.

LATE IN THE NIGHT the cats took up meowing, nearing a howl. Geneva and Cheri heard them at the same moment—Geneva lying on top of the covers of the mattress she slept on and Cheri tucked tightly into her childhood single bed. Both of them left their windows open a crack each night to get the fresh air. It's what Auntie Marie always taught them to do.

They assumed the cats would let up after a bit but when they did not, they each got up from bed, slipped on clothes and shoes, and made their way out to see what was agitating the animals. Could be a hungry fox or a coyote, but one of them surely wouldn't be stupid enough to take on the wild cats.

Cheri walked to the back door of the house with a flashlight and found Geneva already waiting. They nodded to each other and walked out, side by side. As they neared the shed, Cheri turned on the flashlight and pointed it in the direction of the noise. Dozens of pairs of gleaming eyes shone back, open mouths, swishing tails.

There was no coyote, no fox. Cats weren't warring with each other either. It was something else: Auntie Marie was dead. They both felt she was dead before they knew it for sure. They would find her later in bed, mouth agape, hands and feet like ice. But for the moment there were the cats crying, the chill breeze rattling the remaining leaves.

"Why didn't you make her get treatment?" Cheri asked, shutting off her light and looking up at the sky, the moon.

"Why didn't you?" Geneva stepped away, headed in the direction of the woods.

"I wasn't here," Cheri said.

"Right," Geneva said over her shoulder. "You weren't here."

Cheri followed Geneva's straight, angry back to the woods. They walked in silence with Geneva leading until they found the spot in the clearing. Using the moon's pale light, they gathered up leaves, twigs, and larger branches and set them down in the fire round. Geneva pulled a lighter out of her pocket and bent over the pile. She lit the lighter but could not make it catch.

"I need help," she said. Cheri knelt down beside Geneva and cupped a hand over the flame. The flame caught and they both bent to blow on it in unison until the fire was in good shape. They sat back a ways from the round, close enough to each other that their cross-legged knees could have touched.

"What do we do now?"

"About what?" Geneva rubbed her nose with the clutched sleeve of her shirt.

"With the cats and everything?" Cheri poked at the fire with a stick.

"The ASPCA could help trap them. Get them to a shelter."

"Those cats can't live in a shelter. They're wild. They need to be able to come and go," Cheri said.

"What am I supposed to do with them? I can't do it all myself. Not like this." Geneva turned, faced Cheri and waited until Cheri turned to her, looked. Then she lifted the small stub of arm she still had left and flapped it in Cheri's direction.

Cheri lowered her eyes and Geneva felt a moment of satisfaction. Felt she had gotten through. Cheri would stay. It was what Auntie Marie had hoped. She wanted the two of them to live there, to take over the store, the cats. It must have been her dying wish and Geneva was relieved that it was going to come true.

"I guess we could shoot them," Cheri said. She would not be trapped so easily. She stood up from the fire and left Geneva sitting where she was.

THE TOWN TURNED OUT for the wake and funeral. Auntie Marie was a hero, a saint for facing her cancer the way she did. People praised her for not taking treatment, for going out the way she wanted, for waiting for her miracle.

After she was buried in the ground before it froze up for good, Cheri and Geneva were left to figure out next steps. They'd both been left the store and property, but it was decided that Geneva would stay and work it on her own.

They would shoot the cats together.

THE CATS KEPT UP THEIR RACKET every night in the week after Auntie Marie died. Never letting up, or letting go. Geneva was sure they knew that they would soon die. That Cheri, in her selfish need to flee, would kill them.

On the day Cheri was leaving, they set out to kill the cats with Auntie Marie's rifle. She'd taught them both to shoot when they were young because if there was going to be a gun in the house then everyone should know how to use it properly, to respect it. They were unclear whether Geneva would be able to shoot, but they were willing to give it a try as she'd always been the better shot and neither one wanted to see the cats needlessly suffer because of bad aim.

That day, the sky was a ghostly, pale blue with tufts of milkweed suspended in the air. A lingering flock of geese flew overhead, their V small and haphazard, not like the larger flocks that had flown over in August. It was time to head south or risk spending the winter in the cold, foodless north. Cheri felt this, too, and could barely conceal her eagerness to get this over with, shoot the cats, and leave it all behind.

She realized that this might be the last time she saw any of it. Saw Geneva. Here was a thought that both pleased and horrified her. She had become a person who could easily walk away from her responsibilities. She was not the person her aunt had raised. This much was clear.

"Well," Geneva said as they stood before the shed. "I guess we might as well do it now." She raised the butt of the rifle to her shoulder, and took aim. The gun slipped. Geneva dropped her head and handed it over to Cheri. "I can't do it," she said. "It's too shaky."

Cheri took the rifle, lifted it, and aimed. The cat she chose first was a sleek black Tom with white paws and a white diamond on his forehead. She put her finger on the trigger and eased it back. The cat stared at her. Opened its mouth wide, but no sound came out.

She felt it knew it was about to die. It did not run, even though that is the most important instinct living creatures have—to run when in danger. The cat flicked its head and lifted a paw to its mouth, licked it, and then swiped it over its face.

Cheri lowered the gun from shooting position and placed it on the ground. She had seen the face of her Auntie Marie in that cat and she could not kill it. Could not, in fact, kill anything. Geneva had killed before—rats that got into the shed, a rabid raccoon—but Cheri had never been able to. "You don't have the stomach for it," is what Auntie Marie said when they were growing up and Cheri choked at the rifle time and again. "You've got too much of your mother in you. Just a tender heart with black all around the edges where your bad side fights your good side."

"I can't do it," Cheri said when it seemed the silence might rise up and pull her into the sky.

"I know," Geneva said and let her right hand snake out to find Cheri's left one, which she grabbed, squeezed tight, and then let go.

3

RENEE FELT THE COMING RUSH of customers like Harley motors thrumming down the highway. It was 4:30 when she and Rick took over from the early shift at Titty's Bar and Grille and got ready for the long night ahead. They were partners in everything, she and Rick, and had been for going on two years, which is why Jimmy Titty wanted the two of them behind the bar of his establishment. "Y'all've got my back," he said on more than one occasion. "I know y'all do." And sure they did, but that didn't mean that every once in a while some cash didn't get slipped into a pocket instead of a register or that a bottle of beer didn't get opened and drunk and never paid for.

Tending bar was hard to live on as an hourly wage—even counting tips—and New Smyrna Beach didn't bring in your spring breakers or snow birds so much as a Daytona or a West Palm did. She and Rick needed that extra cash. Hell, they deserved it. They could've moved on—had the chance many times—but New Smyrna was home, and Titty's was family, and family helped you out no matter what.

What brought Renee to Florida was not so much a love of

warm weather and palm trees as it was a need to be as far away from where she came from as she could imagine. But why New Smyrna Beach in particular?

The answer was simple: Bike Week. The first time she set foot in Florida was when she and her then-boyfriend rode into town on his Harley during Bike Week. The sense of immediate inclusion was like nothing she had felt before. No one gave a shit if she drank half a dozen shots a night or snorted a little something every once in a while. No one cared that she'd left her kid behind to be raised by her sister. No one cared that she barely knew Blackie before she got on the back of that bike. No one cared about anything at all other than getting messed up and having a good time doing it. And when she learned that Bike Week wasn't just a one-time thing, she was sold.

In fact, Bike Week happened every year, rain or shine, and the heart of Bike Week was New Smyrna Beach and the ventricles were the many bars dotting the road leading to and from the beach. Bike Week was exciting, it was different, and, in the end, it was something to live for—that week in March when folks from all over would want to be right where she was. Right there. Sure, it wasn't as big as Sturgis but it was big enough, man. It was big enough. And Titty's Bar and Grille was the beating bloody pulse of the heart of Bike Week. It was everything.

A few months on, the bar would be packed already with bikers, getting rowdy, slapping ass, looking for trouble. There was no distinction between day and night during Bike Week. It was one long kick-ass party full of sex and drugs and beer and rock and roll. And thirsty, big-tipping, barrel-chested men on bikes.

But now was the time for prep—the time to mentally and physically ready yourself for the onslaught. Renee had been going to the tanning booth for months in anticipation, and judging from the eyes on her flat, brown belly, if she kept it up, tips would be good that year. She couldn't wait.

She washed the remaining dirty glasses. Wiped down the liquor bottles and waited for Rick to finish loading up the coolers and the ice. "Dang ice machine is broke again." Rick banged through the swinging door from the back with two cases of Bud, feet squelching on the sticky floor. Renee would need to get the mop out and wash it down before things got busy or else she'd go crazy with her feet sticking to the tiles every time she walked over to get a cold one out of the cooler. "Jimmy's got a call in but who knows when they'll come fix it. I'm going for ice."

Renee nodded. Swiped the bar top with a clean rag, eyed the straggling customers to see if anyone was empty. "All righty," she said. "You do that."

"What?" Rick said, opening one of the coolers and placing beers inside. "I'm getting ice, I said. Ice." He told her he was clean, but she knew different. The past few months he'd been slipping, needing, needling. She comforted herself that at least it wasn't meth he was using—just heroin. Meth would mess you up. Sure, heroin would mess you up, too, but not like meth would. That shit was lethal.

"I know what you said." Renee moved away from him to where a customer held up his glass, rattled the ice cubes.

Rum and coke, honey. Rum and coke.

She watched Rick walk out into the growing dark. Late-to-nest birds canvassed the dusky sky above the parking lot, swooping like feeding bats on a summer night, out of light, out of light.

There didn't seem to be as many bats in Florida as there were back home. At least not near the ocean. Could be that the constant wind kept them away, or maybe it was the open space with nothing to bounce sound off but air and sand. Not like in the mountains, among the piney woods, flying low above the lake—sound echoed endlessly there, sound upon sound. She thought of the twilight sky at home and saw it as one mass of bat bodies, black and flapping, winged, moving forward, pushing away, pursuing.

ONCE SHE'D BEEN AT A HOUSE of bats with a man whose name she could no longer remember. It was not his house, but the summerhouse of his parents, both dead. He was there to clean it out, get it ready for sale. He did not live there. No one lived at the lake then. No one stayed past the time the last leaf dropped. She had sex with him in the bedroom of this A-frame on the shore of the lake.

The structure was painted red and roofed in wood shingles. The bats, he told her, live beneath the shingles. He motioned for her to watch out the window as the sun set over the distant mountains.

You'll see them soon, he said. Watch.

It had felt good to be lying in the crook of his arm, hand on chest. It felt good to be told to watch as though she were someone worthy of watching when others commanded. She'd told her sister she had something important to take care of but really all she had to do was come to the house of this man she'd met when he stopped in at the store for supplies. He had written directions for her. Told her he'd cook dinner.

It wasn't until she got to the house that she remembered he'd not bought any real food, only beer and coffee. A box of donuts. A roll of toilet paper. Matches. But he had pot and music. Soon they kissed.

Relax, he said. We're cool.

She was relaxed. She was cool. She wanted to be there.

They watched and saw one black dot grow smaller in the twilight, and then another and another. It was spring and the window was open to let in a chill breeze. Small waves lapped the shore, tinkling the late remaining ice. They heard wind in the new green leaves. Once in a while, they heard the high-pitched squeak of a bat. The bodies grew frequent, indistinguishable one from the other. She reached her hand out in the direction of the window as if to grab hold of them and let them pull her out into the sky and share their night with her.

He got out of bed and dressed, went downstairs. She followed and took a sip from a sticky beer bottle on the coffee table, unsure if it was hers. He yawned and stretched, looked at his watch. She told him she had things to do.

Yes, he said. You better go.

He turned the porch light on for her and stepped out. She hesitated at the door, foot pushing against the screen, not yet ready to give up the potential of more time in this house with him, pretending it was where she lived and that he was her husband, or, at the very least, her boyfriend. The day had been warm but the night air was cold on her skin, still blushed and mottled from the friction of their bodies rubbing together. She wrapped her arms across her chest and stepped out onto the porch.

His back was to her when she noticed the thing at her feet, furry and brown, impossibly small. She nudged it with her toe and it flexed its wings. She felt she should do something before he turned around and noticed it. He had the look of cruelty about him—tightness in his lips, the linger of a smirk.

He saw the bat before she even noticed he was looking.

Hang on, he said. Don't move.

He went inside and came back with a trowel in hand. He bent and smashed the head, then scooped the small body onto the blade, walked to the edge of the woods, and flung it far into the darkness. They did not even hear it land.

He walked back to her and leaned on the railing. He had no choice, he said. It could have been rabid, dangerous. A dog might have found it and eaten it.

It's not good to take chances, he said.

Driving home in the pitch dark, she watched the telephone wires for the lights of oncoming cars to know when to switch off her high beams. Sometimes she would switch off her lights entirely, wait for the car to pass and switch them back on. She knew the road home the way a bat knew the sky.

RENEE THOUGHT SHE HAD GOOD INSTINCTS. She had, in fact, on more than one occasion called herself a good judge of character. The regulars at Titty's knew different, though. To them, she was childlike, naïve, a collector of broken things: sea glass, stubs of pencils, sticky-eyed cats, and men like Rick who would never take to the fixing she so wanted to give them. It was easy for everyone who saw them together to know that Rick, a younger man—handsome enough to head down to Miami Beach and rub noses with the beautiful people—was playing her, that his protestations of staying off drugs were nothing more than protestations. And though she didn't like it, she accepted it because Rick had never been bad to her, had hardly ever hit or yelled at her. And from the looks of her—wide-eyed, easy to smile at men of all ages—you could tell she always had accepted it from men. All it took was a "sorry" or an "I need you" to get her back on track with guys like Rick.

Renee had been able to handle the bar on her own but things were picking up by the time Rick showed his face. She noted that he came in through the back door and not the front door as he would usually do, even though Jimmy had warned them time and again that he preferred his staff to come in through the rear. "Looks more proper that way," he said. Though some might wonder why there was a need for propriety in an establishment like Titty's, where on your typical night anything went.

Rick stood next to her and squinted into her face. His eyes looked not right—not high, necessarily, more scared, or wild. She reached a hand to touch his arm. Her heart picked up pace. "What's wrong, baby?"

"Come on in back," he said. "For a sec." Then he smiled and she saw that he was excited. The only time Rick was excited was when he was about to get high or when he was scheming how to get rich.

"We've got customers, baby," Renee said.

"One second," he said. "Please, baby." He swung back through the door and she followed, more out of curiosity than any desire to be involved in whatever he had going. She was tired, still getting over a lingering sinus infection, and the night already seemed to have gone on too long. She needed to be in good health for Bike Week, that much was true.

Rick led the way to the liquor storage room, which they typically kept locked at all times. He jingled his keys to find the one that opened the padlock, inserted it, turned and opened the lock. He looked back over his shoulder and smiled a smile that said, *wait until you see this.*

On the floor, in the tepid beam of light, was a baby—five months old if a day—sleeping in its car seat. Renee's breasts tingled as she thought of her own baby all those years ago. Thought of the day her milk came in and her sister helped her get the baby to latch on. "How do you even know about this stuff?" she had asked her childless sister Marie, who answered, "Who do you think helped your mother with you?"

For a wild second she believed this baby in front of her was her baby—her Cheri—come back to her. Traveled forward in time and miles and miles to where she was. She longed to pick the child up and hold her close, rest her chin on the soft crown of the head, breathe in the scent of her cradle cap.

"We're going to be rich," Rick said. "Rich."

———

WHEN RENEE LEFT THE NORTH, she left with a man who went by the name Blackie. He had stopped at the store to fill up his Harley. Traveled cross-country, he said. Hit Sturgis in the summer and then he'd holed up in Minnesota for a while. "Good fishing," he said, winking at her as he leaned on the counter, every once in a while lurching forward to gape down at her legs, long and shapely below her cut offs. "Headed down south now," he said. "Make a few stops along the way before I hit New Smyrna for Bike Week." It all sounded so glamorous—travel, living here and there, no worries, no complications. She didn't ask him how he afforded it all. Didn't care.

"Want to join me?" he said, and Renee, without thinking, said yes, though she'd not even known his name at that point. When she quietly reminisced about this story she told herself it had not been an easy choice to leave Cheri behind the way she did. She told herself that it was in her daughter's best interest that she live with Marie, who would raise Cheri the same way she had raised Renee. That Cheri stay in the house where Renee had grown up. That Cheri learn the way of the store and the town and of the people who could be bad, but were often good.

Renee believed that by leaving Cheri behind, she had saved the child's life. It was no kind of life for a kid to live with a mother who worked six nights a week and partied on the seventh. In her dark heart, she knew the truth, though. She hadn't wanted to be a mother anymore. She wanted to be free, to travel without restriction. To not have to care about anyone else but herself—and even then, to not have to care about herself. That was the best of all.

She could no longer remember what Blackie's real name was or why it was she loved him so. A con artist by trade, he had been cruel to her, merciless in his beatings, and unquenchable in his desire for other women. But she believed there was something special about him, something broken, damaged. He needed her and she could help him in a way she could no longer help her own child. Once Cheri moved from infant to child, she no longer needed Renee.

She remembered Cheri's face when she told her she would be staying behind with Marie. How the child took in the information and reacted briefly with upset, but then calmed down and took her dose of reality.

When Renee visited after that on her saved up tips from cocktail waitressing and eventually bartending, Cheri's reaction tapered down and down until it seemed she had forgotten that Renee had ever been her mother. And so she stopped visiting entirely. It seemed better that way. Easier for them all.

Of course, Marie sent her chastising notes, saying "this child needs her mother" and such, but Renee knew otherwise. She'd done without her mother at that age and Cheri could do as well. It would toughen her up, make her stronger. She hoped that the adult Cheri now realized what a sacrifice her mother had made for her. How her mother had saved her life.

THE CUSTOMERS PICKED UP steady from eight until midnight and Renee hustled as best she could with Rick doing part time. Every twenty minutes or so he scooted back to the liquor room to check on the baby while Renee manned the front.

The baby. Rick had a plan for the baby. He didn't want to go into too many details but he said he knew people who would pay good money for a baby, especially one with all of its fingers and toes and other working parts. Especially for such a pretty little girl. Good money.

Oh, he was happy at the thought of the money he would make on this baby. "We'll make twenty grand—easy. Maybe even thirty. Take a couple of months off, work on getting my shop up and running." His dream was to open a motorcycle repair shop, but there was apparently never enough money or time for this fantasy to come to fruition. Renee did wonder given all the money and time whether Rick would follow through on it anyway. She pictured the money flying away as quickly as it landed. She pictured Rick in their trailer, sitting on the couch in front of *Judge Judy* on the tube, his arm outstretched beside him with the needle still dangling from the tender part in the crook of the elbow.

Later, when all of the customers left or had been kicked out and the doors were locked, they sat drinking a beer at the bar, the quiet baby in her car seat on a stool between them. Renee thought to fix up a bottle with some of the milk they used for White Russians but she worried that there wasn't any formula. She didn't think the baby should have milk so early. She remembered Marie telling her something about babies and allergies. She decided to hold off on giving her the milk—she didn't want to make matters worse than they already were.

The baby smelled rank.

When Renee asked Rick how the baby came to be in his possession his answers were vague, until finally he admitted that Mittens, one of his old clients and ex-girlfriends from back when he had been more dealer than user, had given the baby to him. "She owed me big time," Rick said, "but this more than pays off her debt." He reached out and clucked the baby under the chin. Renee fought hard not to knock his hand away. He'd not washed since counting out their tips. The germs from the money alone were enough to make the infant sick.

She stood and snatched the baby up to her chest, feeling the weight of her lumpy diaper in the hand that held her bottom. The baby had not once whimpered, and this alone made Renee want to cry.

"What's her name?" Renee bounced her knees to keep the baby in motion, calm.

"She was going to be called Catherine," Rick said, "but Mittens said that was too grown up of a name for a baby so she called her Cree instead."

"We need to get going," Renee said. "Got to find a store that's open so we can get some diapers and formula."

"Chill out, baby. I got some of that stuff in the car," Rick said. "Mittens gave it to me."

"Go on and get it, then," Renee said. "Cree's got a stinky load in her pants." Rick left and came back with a plastic grocery bag inside of which was an extra bottle of formula, now tepid and likely spoiled from having sat out all night, and three diapers. Renee sighed and brought the baby back to the staff bathroom that seemed cleaner than the customer one at this point in the evening.

She'd brought a couple of clean bar towels with her, which she laid down on the floor, and then she gently put Cree down upon them. It was the first time she and the baby had been alone. Renee took the opportunity to look, to take in. The baby smiled, showing off her pale pink gums. "How could anyone ever give you away?" she said and then covered her mouth in her own foolishness.

She knew how it was to give a child away. But not a baby. Never a baby. She'd waited, at least, until Cheri was more self-sufficient. Renee had always been a sucker for babies. So tiny and helpless, the need so apparent in their every move. She craved to be needed this way, but it was so fleeting. There and then gone. Until finally you learned that no one ever really needed you. That you are all alone when it really counts.

She ran her index finger over the velvet skin of Cree's face. The cheeks were perhaps gaunter than you would want, and there was a bluish tint under the eyes. The baby's body was listless. Renee sensed she was not well.

"Let's get you cleaned up," Renee said and lifted the soft feet clothed in filthy socks as she undid the onesie. All of the years had not squelched her memory of how to change a diaper. It's something you never forgot how to do once you'd done it a thousand times or so. Inside, the fecal matter was scant, a single explosion of green. The urine dark yellow. Things were not right. They might have to go to the hospital and then what? Neither one of them had insurance, not to mention could prove that this was their own child.

She pictured the scene at the hospital, how she would be forceful with the nurses that Cree get special care. How she would object to their charges of neglect. But if there was neglect, if the baby was found to be undernourished as surely she would be, then social services would be called in. The police. Not good.

Of course there were no wipes in the bag, so Renee did her best with harsh brown paper towels and water. The baby changed her facial expression slightly at the feeling of the towel on her skin but she did not cry. "Sorry," Renee said. "I'll do better next time." It was a sorry-ass clean up but it would have to do. Renee snapped the onesie back up and lifted the baby to her chest. She kissed the top of Cree's head and breathed in the scent, soured with neglect but unmistakably baby. She clenched her legs together with the urgency of her feelings. Tears. A baby.

Later she left Rick in the car while she went into the 24-hour Publix and bought diapers and wipes and formula and even a few jars of food just in case. On a whim, she picked up a few terry cloth toys and tub toys. The next day, she'd get a diaper bag and more supplies, some proper clothes.

As she left the store, she realized that she was smiling.

———

THEY LIVED TOGETHER at Lazy Palms trailer park. The place had been Renee's to begin with but Rick had moved in with her after the first night they were together. That night lasted until morning and then even in the morning they could not get enough of each other. The sex had been exquisite at first but soon Rick started using again and things fell apart. This was the pattern every six months or so and now that they were preparing for Bike Week and had the baby on their hands, he was about due again to implode.

Usually at times like this, Renee kept a nervous eye on him, but now, with the baby, she forgot to worry over Rick. She was bone tired and wanted to get this child settled and then get some rest herself, but Rick wanted to discuss his plan. He knew people, he said, who could help them out, find a buyer. All the while he was talking, Renee watched the baby, sleeping soundly in the drawer she'd fixed up for a bassinette. Renee kept one hand flat on her own belly the whole time, feeling for sure what she needed to do.

Finally, when Rick laid back against his pillow and smiled up at the low ceiling, so proud of his genius, she'd climbed on top of him. "I want you," she said.

Rick sat up halfway, leaning on his elbows. "What about the baby?"

"She's sleeping," Renee said. "Won't even notice."

He settled back down and smiled up at her. "Okay," he said, nodding, rubbing his palms together. "All right." He reached a hand over to the nightstand, but she grabbed it back and put it on her tanned breast, which she'd slipped out of her tank top.

"No," she said. "I want to feel you tonight." It was risky, she knew, to not use a condom with him, but it was also an opportunity. For a while she'd been playing around with the idea of having another baby while she still had the chance. She didn't know what Rick's feelings on the matter would be but she didn't care either. The introduction of the baby only heightened her desire for another child of her own. She kept trying, though in her heart she knew Rick was no more capable of fathering a child than he was of staying clean. She refused to believe that the problem might be her own even though the last doctor she'd seen had told her that pregnancy might no longer be an option for her. "Your ovaries are cystic," the doctor informed her. "Conception is possible, but will be difficult."

"Yeah?" Rick said.

"Yeah," she said, and undid her jeans, slid them off and took his penis in hand.

Cree slept the entire time, but Renee could not keep her mind off how it had felt to hold that small body next to hers. Her baby.

EVEN THOUGH HER OWN DAUGHTER was now grown, Renee was still a young woman herself—not yet forty and didn't look a day over thirty, she thought. This child easily could have been her own. She liked the feeling of having Cree safely strapped in her car seat in the back, Renee up front driving around in the bright of day like a normal person—just a mother out with her child, on their way shopping.

At the store, Renee charged several cute outfits—pink and clean. Socks, diapers, formula, bottles, an umbrella stroller, blankets, and towels. A couple of times older women stopped Renee and asked questions or made comments. How old was the baby and wasn't she just the sweetest thing and wasn't she just daddy's little girl. Renee absorbed the attention until she became worried that folks might get too nosy. That she and Cree might end up on some surveillance camera or that they would bump into someone who knew Renee. It was time to go. She needed to get back and get ready for her shift at Titty's. They still hadn't figured out a plan for how they would work it with the baby yet. Renee could call in sick, but then she'd never done that—not even when she really was sick. Jimmy might get suspicious, ask questions. He was the paranoid sort and always worried that Renee would leave him to go work for a rival. "You know you're the only man for me, Jimmy," Renee said time and again.

Rick suggested they leave the baby with his mother, but Renee nixed that plan. "Woman can't even change her own Depends let alone take care of this little one's diaper." They decided that Renee would drop Rick off early and then come in later with the baby, when there was no chance that Jimmy might be there. By seven every night he was home in front of his HDTV watching *Jeopardy*. They'd keep the baby in back in the liquor room. If push came to shove and they had to answer to Jimmy, Renee figured she'd tell him she was watching the baby for her cousin, who was in trouble. Like Renee, Jimmy had a soft spot for folks in trouble, particularly young women who looked like Renee.

But first things first, she needed to get the child home, bathed, and fed. The baby's bowel movements were still an alarming consistency but Renee figured with a few days of proper care things would get better. They had to.

SHE REMEMBERED THE DAY Cheri was born and how her shame of having a baby at sixteen, unwed and unwanted, was immediately eclipsed by the brightness of the love she felt for her daughter. It was as though she was also loving herself for the first time—or recognizing who she was, and who she would be. A woman, a mother, one who loves deeply. And forever.

When she held Cheri in her arms at the hospital on that first day, she had felt for the first time her purpose for being alive. This was it. This baby. The baby nuzzled at her breast, pushed its face against her skin. The baby knew her. Knew Renee was her mother. This was the need she was meant to fill. This.

She wanted that feeling to stay forever, but as Cheri aged and Renee realized that her life was slipping away, the feeling had waned until it finally dissipated, only to tug at her here and there. Now she wanted it back. Would, in fact, do just about anything to get it: If she couldn't have her own baby, then someone else's baby would do just fine.

THE LONGER THEY HAD THE BABY, the healthier she became and also the more time and attention she demanded of them. Rick became impatient with how much time Renee was spending in the backroom each night, rocking and singing to the baby. He winced every time he watched her holding the baby on the couch at home, her arm bent protectively inward, the child lifting its fingers up to grasp for her breasts, her hair. "We can't keep her, you know," he said when he watched Renee and the baby. At times, Renee wondered if he was jealous—the thought of which secretly thrilled her—though she never would have wanted to cause him harm.

"We're going to have to move on the plan," Rick said, after a particularly trying night in which the baby refused to fall asleep in the liquor room without Renee first rocking her for an hour. Renee nodded but she wasn't yet sure what the plan was, exactly, other than some nameless, faceless people who would buy the baby.

"Don't you think we should wait a little longer?" Renee said, running her hand up and down his bare thigh. She was hoping Rick would become as taken with the baby as she was. That the baby would stay with them, be their child.

"We've got to move. We don't want Mittens to get restless and want her back," Rick said. "Besides, folks are starting to get fishy." Rick claimed one of their neighbors had seen them loading the baby into the car. "She looked at us funny," he said. "Like she knew something wasn't right." Rick stretched his arms up straight, cracked the knuckles. "Anyway, we can't have that thing hanging around forever. Won't fly during Bike Week. Won't fly at all."

Renee rolled over onto her side, her back to Rick as he talked on about his plan. She watched the rise and fall of the baby's chest, fast asleep in the Pack 'n Play she'd bought at the consignment store. Her own plan started to form. North was where they would go. Back home. The baby would be safe there and so would she. She knew that Marie would take them in and, hopefully, agree to raise the child as she had raised so many others. She wouldn't call Marie to let her know they were coming; it would be too easy for Marie to refuse them. Instead Renee would write a letter to soften her sister up. She thought of Marie and Cheri watching her from the plate glass window of the store as she and Cree pulled into the parking lot. Thought of their faces, first cold at the sight of a stranger, turning quickly to joy at her homecoming. Renee pictured her daughter as she herself had been at twenty-two, still fresh-faced and guileless. Open to love and the world.

Soon Rick slept soundly beside her. He would not wake. He never woke. Every day it was a fight to get him roused in time to shower before work. She made out Cree's shape where she slept, smelled the familiar scent of the baby's breath.

There hadn't been room in the bedroom for all of the baby's things. They were safely tucked away in the main room. From the back of the jammed closet, Renee pulled out a flattened duffle bag, which she stuffed full of underwear and socks, some t-shirts, jeans, the one warm sweatshirt she owned. She took half the carton of cigarettes on the dresser and left the rest for Rick. He would need them when he realized she and the baby were gone. Hell, she figured she'd be in Virginia by the time he woke up.

Out in the main room she reached up onto the top shelf where they stored their videocassettes and pulled down *On Golden Pond*—a favorite of hers, but one that Rick abhorred. The case was stuffed with all of the money, changed to hundreds, she'd been hoarding from Rick so that he wouldn't use it for drugs.

She loaded the car and then went back in for the baby. As she picked up Cree, Rick changed positions on the bed. "What's wrong?" he said.

"Diaper needs changing," Renee whispered. Rick had agreed to give a bottle or two but he drew the line at changing diapers.

"Be back in a minute," she said and bent over to kiss him on the forehead. Then she stood in the spot until she heard his breathing turn to sleep again. Renee left the room, the trailer, got into the car and drove north. Away from Rick, a man she would have once died for. Away from Titty's Bar and Grille, her heart tugging at the thought of missing out on Bike Week. Away from Volusia County, a place that had been home to her all these many years since leaving the north.

She thought she would feel more at the leaving of all of it, but realized it felt less painful than had she decided to go the convenience store for a pack of smokes. It was behind her. She would miss Rick, but now she had Cree to worry about. She couldn't let him sell the baby to the highest bidder. This was a living, breathing human baby. The people who bought her might not love her, or worse, they might have some other, more nefarious plans. Every day you heard horrible, disgusting stories of what people did to their own babies. What would they do if the baby wasn't even their own flesh and blood?

Renee could not bear to think about it. If she could have saved all the babies of the world, she would have.

They pulled off for breakfast at a truck stop north of Jacksonville, right before they crossed the border into Georgia. Coffee and a smoke for Renee, formula and a diaper change for Cree. In the gift store, Renee bought a card and a stamp. She set Cree's car seat down at one of the picnic tables in the grassy bit by the side of the building and wrote out a letter to Marie. With any luck it would reach her sister before she did. After posting it, they drove on.

"We're going up north," Renee said aloud, not sure whether Cree slept or not in her car seat. "You'll see snow and bats flying over the lake at dusk. You'll smell the balsam. You'll hear the ice moaning in the spring when it cracks apart." There was no end of things Cree would learn about up north. It would be her home.

Renee would tell them all that Cree was her child. She would tell Marie that Cree was her niece. She would tell Cheri that Cree was her sister. It would all work out. They were a family.

4

THE AIR WAS SHARP with frost not yet burned off by the low sun as Geneva walked to the mailbox. Gray trees along the roadside creaked in the wind, bare branches scratching out the blue from the sky. A single crow let out a continuous, ornery caw, rippling the morning's stillness. She wasn't sure why she bothered to collect the mail at all. The box would be loaded with bills—for stock, for dairy, for newspapers and magazines, for heat and electric that kept the store warm and buzzing. At first it seemed the perfect legacy that Auntie Marie left the store to Cheri and her, but now the reality of the situation—no money in the till and less each day as the convenience store in town gained popularity, back taxes and bills piling up—left her feeling as though she were skating for the first time and couldn't get her feet to move in the same direction so that time and again she ended up on her ass. And though she had agreed to stay and help out, Cheri was nothing but an added burden—out all night, sleeping off a hangover during the day. Geneva had to prod her to do the bare minimum.

She would have thought that life with Clint where they were always one step ahead of the bill collectors would have prepared her for this new life of want, but it hadn't. Things should have been easier.

Geneva thought she might pray on her troubles the way Auntie Marie taught her to when she first took her in. "You don't have to kneel at the side of your bed or in a church pew," is what Auntie Marie said. "All you've got to do is think heavenly thoughts and send your messages up to God. You can do that anywhere." Auntie Marie prayed all the time, even while she worked the till. Hell, she even prayed at Bingo—but never so that she would win, only that her girls were safe and healthy, only that they were warm and educated. Only that God save her from cancer by some miracle—but only if she was worthy of saving. Only then. But God hadn't saved her. He had other plans for Auntie Marie—that she might become a martyr for the older townsfolk to worship. No medicine for her. No, sir. If prayer couldn't cure her, then neither could doctors.

The packet of mail was thick in Geneva's hand. When she was going through the motions of daily life and not thinking about her lost arm at all, her brain would think about doing something like opening the mail, say, and SLAM, she would realize that short of ripping it open with her teeth, she simply couldn't do it with just her one hand.

Couldn't do it. Words she was learning to live by. At the hospital they had talked to her about a prosthetic arm, but she had said no. She wanted her old arm back or nothing at all.

She would have to wait until she was inside to open the mail, but for now she wedged the packet against her belly and used her fingers to flick through and see what she had to look forward to. Bills, bills, bills, bills, and something else: a letter. Not just any letter, but what felt like a card encased in a cheap pink envelope. A letter addressed to Marie. The name on the return address? Renee—Marie's sister, Cheri's mother.

Not even so much as a Christmas card from Renee had made

its way into the mailbox before this pink envelope. Geneva supposed they all figured she was dead, but she couldn't know for sure; maybe Auntie Marie and Cheri had different information, squirreled away for their eyes only. Geneva wasn't a blood relative after all—only a foster kid who stuck for good. "You're like a burr, girl," is what Auntie Marie said when she was younger and questioning how long she would get to stay, "I couldn't get rid of you without digging you out good."

She supposed she was something like a prickly burr, clinging to your sock after you walked through the field on an autumn afternoon, dangling there unnoticed, waiting to stick to your fingers when you pulled off your shoes at night so that you would never forget it. I exist. I am here and it's going to take some work on your part to get rid of me.

Renee was the opposite of a burr: She clung to nothing save her vanity. Renee was soft, light, and perhaps a little bit stupid. Or maybe she wanted you to believe that about her—that she was guileless. Geneva had never gotten close enough to know for sure. Whenever Renee came around it was to see Cheri, to crowd onto her, hug her, kiss her, play the good mother. Leaving Geneva and Auntie Marie gripped with fear that this would be the time Cheri would be taken away from them for good.

But that never happened and eventually Cheri stopped crying about it. "She's a narcissist is what she is," Cheri said after the last time her mother came and went. Geneva and Cheri were out smoking by the campfire, drinking beers and listening to the peepers by the brook. "All she cares about is herself. Not me. And that's fine because I don't care if I ever see or hear from her again." Geneva wanted to believe what Cheri was saying, that she didn't care, but she couldn't quite buy it. Geneva's own mother had given her away like an unwanted puppy yet when they'd taken Geneva from her,

Geneva believed her mother's heart still broke from the separation. It was those few moments when a mother showed a child love that she missed—those desperate, hopeful moments that meant you were important to someone in this world.

Back behind the counter in the store, Geneva pulled the card from the stack to examine it. The postmark said Florida. Pink flamingoes, palm trees, sand between your toes, and Disney. Geneva had never been to Florida. She sniffed the envelope. It smelled of rust and damp from the mailbox.

She held it up to the light but could make out only words on top of words, covering and crossing each other on thin paper. Before she knew what she was doing, Geneva had the card on the counter and was opening it. Renee was thinking about coming home, she said. "Keep an eye out," the note said. "I'll be there sooner than you think."

Not even signed with love, but hugs and kisses. Not surprising, though, because hugs and kisses were easy and love was hard, especially for folks like Renee.

The buzzer sounded. A customer out at the pumps. Geneva stuffed the card beneath the counter and used her sleeve to wipe a clean a patch on the steamy window.

Clint was filling up his truck. He could have gone anywhere for gas, why'd he have to mess with her? Of course, the pumps were the old kind where you had to come in and pay with cash. Not that Clint had any credit that wasn't maxed out anyway.

She didn't want him to catch her seething behind the counter, waiting on him when he came in, so she busied herself dusting the already dust-free cans of cling peaches, green beans, and peas on the shelves in the middle of the store. Soon she would have to do inventory of the stock and see what she really needed more of and what she could get by on. She poked a bag of marshmallows with her finger and found them turning hard.

The bell on the door jingled Clint's entrance.

"G'day there," Clint called out. Her skin went hot at the sound of his voice. She clenched her fists. Her fist. One. But it still felt like two.

"I heard you," Geneva said. She picked up a can of peas and weighed it in her palm, considered turning and pegging it at him, satisfied at the thought of the tin thunking against his skull. "Put your money on the counter and be gone with you."

"Alls I got's a twenty and the gas was $3.84."

"Three-eighty-four?" Geneva turned around, can in hand. "Why'd you stop here if you weren't down to fumes?" Clint's eyes were on her hand, the can. She looked down to see her knuckles whitening. She placed the peas back on the shelf and moved to the register. "Let's be done with this."

Clint walked to the counter and pulled out his wallet. She watched him paw through the crinkled bills and saw plenty smaller than twenties. Typical for the liar. "Going down to the southern tier," he said. "Hunting. And you're cheaper than the Quik-n-Go to town. Cheaper by three cents a gallon. Good bargain. You know I like a bargain." He grinned at her, so that Geneva wished she could see her own expression. She hoped it was as hard and unfathomable as she was willing it to be. "You ought to get some of that flavored coffee they got. Some hazelnut. Irish Cream. Put some donuts out, maybe? Brighten the place up a bit. Make it more welcoming."

Clint handed her the twenty and she made change. She placed the coins first in his palm and was moved by the feel of his skin beneath the pads of her fingers. It's true the feeling in her existing hand had become hypersensitive since the accident, since the loss of her other arm, as though the touch of both hands had doubled into one. She dropped the rest of the change without counting and pressed the bills in after.

"There you go," she said.

"Geneva..."

"I've got work to do." She certainly hoped Clint knew better than to try to talk to her when she didn't want talking to. They'd been together a long time and apart for a short one, but the apart time seemed more keen, more real than the time together.

Clint left without another word. She watched him get back in his truck and pull out onto the road. She thought of the two of them sitting side by side in that truck on their wedding day. How she had felt there was so much promise between them—a life filled with children and nights by the fire. Of love and devotion and never fear. Never. But that had only lasted so long. Clint was never meant to stay cooped up in a house with her. He needed to roam always and she needed to let him go. She was always attracted to these creatures who wanted nothing more than to get away from her. She wanted to learn to love a thing that loved her back. If there even was such a thing.

The skin on her missing arm tingled as Clint's taillights crested the hill and faded out of sight. She didn't think she would ever get over missing him.

CHERI HAD SEEN Clint's truck out front. Watched him fill his tank, enter the store. When he didn't immediately walk back out, she left. Took off walking down the road as she had come to do. A couple of times a week now she walked into town and found herself a seat at the old hotel bar. The rooms above were all closed now, long since gone to seed. Now just the bar was lit and open and someone was always there from the minute it opened until last call early the next morning. Cheri felt comfortable there even though she was not so anonymous as she had been in the city. Some folks recognized her as Marie's kin and said how sorry they were to lose her. Others just stared at the oddness of her—her tattoos, her clothes. And then there were the others—the men and boys who met her eyes and understood what she was about. They were the ones who gave her a ride home at night, dropping her off long after the bar had closed. Mostly she couldn't remember their names or even what they looked like, their breath like weapons on her skin, frightened by the fierceness of her grip as she wrapped her arms and legs around them, maybe even wishing she wouldn't let them go, but she did. As soon as it was over, she was done. "Bring me home," she said.

Usually she took off walking because she was bored and frustrated and because she needed to fill up this gap that was spreading within her until it threatened to swallow her up, but now she walked because she was angry. Of course Geneva would go back with Clint now that Auntie Marie was dead and gone. Of course she would and of course he would ask her to now that she had the store. He was an opportunist. Always had been.

She remembered him when they were younger. At fifteen years old, she was shy and uncomfortable in her skin, so unlike Geneva who radiated ease. But then Clint, beautiful Clint, with his blonde bangs in his eyes and his white teeth—asked her to skate one time in the gym. Her, not Geneva, as she thought he would when he made his way toward them. She did not want to skate with him. Instead she wanted to stay with Geneva, to skate together as they usually did and so she hesitated, pulled back, affected a sulk, but Geneva, beautiful Geneva, said, "Go ahead," and practically pushed her into him.

She felt his arm around her back, holding her up, helping her to move around the circle as others skated by them. One arm around her waist and the other holding her hand. Cheri kept her body far away at first but he pulled her closer so that her side was next to his.

She let herself feel his body next to hers and rested her cheek if not fully on his shoulder, near it. He smelled of hay and rain. Her hand in his grew hot and she feared he would feel the sweatiness of her palm.

When the song ended, he led her back over to where Geneva was standing and smiling. He grabbed Geneva's hand and they skated away. They skated the next three songs after that as well, one slow, one fast and then a final slow one, during which Clint's hand rested comfortably on Geneva's lower back, just above the pockets of her jeans. Geneva seemed to like it there. Cheri stuffed her own hands into her pockets. She would never let a boy touch her there. Ever. She had left the rink and headed home alone, walking fast under a moonless sky. She didn't care how Geneva made it home or if she did at all.

But the next day at breakfast, Geneva was there and on her finger she wore Clint's chunky class ring. "See?" Geneva said twisting her hand around to show Cheri the back of the ring. "I had to wrap string around it. The string will get dirty but I don't care." Geneva talked on about the string and Clint and how great he was and Cheri plotted how she might kill them both or, better yet, how one day she would leave them both behind and become someone worthy of their envy—she would be famous and live in a city and they would only know her through the stories written about her in the newspaper.

And now here she was again back in exactly the same position as she had been that morning so long ago. She'd not been doing much since Auntie Marie died. Hanging out is what she said whenever Geneva asked her what she was up to. She knew Geneva wanted more from her; perhaps she wanted a response that would show she was feeling up to the task of taking care of the store and providing for them as a family, but Cheri had nothing to give.

Up on the side of the road, she saw Terry Plunker parked on his

ATV. She was about to turn and walk the other way when he saw her and waved. She nodded to Plunker as she passed and he got off his ATV to approach her.

It was an odd choice of vehicle, but this was how he got around— he never did get his driver's license or even his permit. Some thought it was because he couldn't pass the reading part, but Plunker could read. In fact, Plunker liked books. The problem was that Plunker was always either too drunk or too hung over to take the test. So he rode his ATV up and down the road, stopping to peer into ditches for redeemable bottles, stopping by some of the houses of richer folks to see if they'd give up theirs. "Got any bottles?" he'd call as he pulled into a driveway. "Any bottles? Gotanybottles?"

"Gotanybottles?" he called to Cheri as she passed.

"Nope," she said. He smiled and got back on his vehicle. Cheri kept her eyes forward on the road ahead.

She thought of Geneva. The summer of their sixteenth year Cheri hardly saw Geneva anymore, as she spent all of her time with Clint, and when she wasn't with Clint, she was talking about him. She recalled that school was out for the day and the mottled May sun had been warm on her back as it broke through the leaves of the trees lining her path to the quarry. Geneva had not been on the bus home, instead she had taken a ride home with Clint. "Tell Marie I'll be home before supper," Geneva said before joining Clint down the hall, away from Cheri. She watched as their bodies met, Clint wrapping a proprietary arm around Geneva before he shuttled her out to the parking lot. Cheri wondered if anyone would ever want her that way—to own her.

She shouldn't think like that. People weren't supposed to want to be owned. She did, though. To be protected, loved, wanted. She should be happy for Geneva. But she wasn't. The jealousy curdled in her stomach day and night, waiting for an opportunity to unleash itself.

Then there was the quarry. A safe haven from Geneva who never went there with her anymore. It became a place where she could go and pretend it belonged to her alone. She'd bushwacked her own path from their property using a topographical map and compass. A perfect secret path that led to the quarry—the place of secrets. She and Geneva swam there often as young girls even though Auntie Marie forbade it. "You get in trouble in there and no one will ever find you," she told them. "Go to town and swim at the rec park with the lifeguard." They went to the quarry specifically because it was off limits. "Let's never come here with anyone else," Geneva said to her once, grasping Cheri's hand in sisterly fondness, holding on to her hand as though to never let go. "It'll be ours alone." Cheri intended on keeping that promise.

Cheri was almost grown and she had lately been giving attention to a feeling that maybe Auntie Marie and Geneva couldn't wait to be rid of her so that they could get on being mother and daughter without her hanging around. She wasn't like them anyway. She'd never be satisfied to stay in this town working at the store. There was more out there for her. Bigger things. Life.

There was no living here, but death and decay and traditions and church and guilt and sadness. Perfect for Geneva who was acting as though she were already married off and having babies. It was depressing.

She heard the voices before she made it out of the woods. Someone else was swimming. Never mind that. She had all day and could wait them out. She would hide and watch and when whoever was there was done swimming, she'd have the place to herself again. As it should be.

She found a spot behind some vegetation and made space for her towel on a smooth rock. She hadn't planned on spying until she heard something familiar: Geneva's laugh echoing off the quarry walls. She had brought Clint here to this secret, sacred place. Cheri thought she might break through the bushes and call out to them, let them know of her presence—let Geneva know that she was aware of this breach of trust.

Instead, she peeked through the bushes at them. There was Clint with his naked back and thighs as he pulled himself up on the rocks. He turned and faced where she hid and she saw the front of him naked—the dark hair surrounding his private parts. Things she had never seen before. She wasn't sure how she was supposed to feel at seeing his penis, probably not repulsed—though she was. Clint reached down and Geneva's hand met his. He pulled her out of the water and Cheri could see that she, too, was naked. She and Geneva had been naked in front of each other hundreds, thousands of times but Cheri had not thought of Geneva this way, with a boy, a man, naked. Clint ran his hands down Geneva's sides and they kissed as his hands found her buttocks and pulled her toward him and down. He sat and Geneva straddled him—her parts on top of his parts.

Cheri watched as their bodies came together and was astonished to find that she wanted this herself—to be a part of them. To be touching and touched by them. She looked around her to make sure no one was there spying her as she spied and then she touched herself as they touched each other. It was wrong, what she was doing, and she hated them because of it and because of it, she loved them.

But that had been a long time ago. Everything had fallen apart and fallen away now. Cheri continued her walk down the road as the sky covered in with clouds and the whine of Plunker's ATV moved away from her. The air was turning dry. It might snow. She thought of the autumn of their last year of school. The entire world was before them, and as Cheri's world expanded with possibility, to Cheri, Geneva's seemed to shrink with commitment and love. "We're going to get married," Geneva whispered to Cheri that night when they were cleaning up the kitchen after dinner, Auntie Marie ensconced in front of the television watching the news.

"Did he propose?" Cheri didn't look up from the plate she was washing. Showed no surprise. Let her face sink into placidity. She knew the best thing to do with Geneva was to pretend you didn't care.

"No," Geneva said, stopping midway through the counter she was wiping. "But I know he will. I'm guessing at Christmas." Geneva smiled, stared past Cheri, out through the window, her mind already in some married place with a husband and children and no Cheri.

In bed that night, Cheri waited for sleep, expected it, wished for it. She wanted sleep to cover her over so that she could stop thinking about Geneva and Clint together at the quarry. During the day she was able to push the images from her mind, but at night when she was alone in her bed, they came back to her as hands—Clint's hands and, worse, they became Geneva's hands, too. These hands were all over her and she tried to wish them away and soon Clint's were gone and all that remained were Geneva's hands on her body.

She was sick and horrible and she must leave this place and leave this black, black piece of her mind behind her. Geneva was her sister. She was not blood but she was as good as blood and to have her hands on Cheri's body even in imagination was disgusting. Auntie Marie would have found her guilty of sin.

But it was dark in her room and no one was there and no one would know and soon Geneva and Clint would be married and their hands would belong to each other alone.

In the years since she'd left, Cheri had done a good job of pushing all those feelings away. But she would be at town soon and there she would find relief from her thoughts. She looked at her hands, red and raw from the wind. When she'd helped clean up her Auntie Marie before the authorities came to take away the body, it was horrible and yet oddly exhilarating seeing her aged aunt naked for the first time—this woman who had pretty much raised her from scratch. The torso and chest lumpy and purpled with tumors was nearly unbearable to view. But worst was the sparse patch of white hair between her auntie's legs.

Cheri recalled rubbing her washcloth over the area, feeling the coarseness of the hair beneath. Instead of disdain, the moment left her feeling connected, rooted.

A hand in a hand is connection. The wind picked up. She listened to it push the branches against each other in agitation.

GENEVA HAD EXPECTED MARRIAGE would allow her to feel protected. Instead it had left her in a constant state of worry. During those days and nights and weeks and weekends of living with Clint, taking care of him, waiting for him to come home, she felt as she had when she was a small girl living with her mother—that instead of being taken care of, she was taking care.

She hadn't minded so much cleaning up after Clint and fixing him meals, it was that he couldn't even do the simplest thing like pay a bill without her. He had come in from collecting the mail during their first month of cohabitation, his cheeks red from the cold and asked her, as he inspected their first electricity bill, "Says pay by check. How do you write one of them anyway?"

"With a pen," she'd said, thinking he was joking, assuming that all grown men knew this simple stuff. Auntie Marie had taught her and Cheri such things early on. Got them to open up bank accounts with their allowance money. Taught them how to save and when to spend.

"You do it then," he said, crumpling up the envelope and throwing it at her where she stood at the kitchen sink washing breakfast dishes. "If you're so damn smart." He left the house, got in the truck and drove away, leaving Geneva to ponder his anger. To wait for his return.

When the afternoon passed and the evening came and he still hadn't returned, her worry increased. She should not have teased him. She'd been unkind and now she was alone because he had left her for good. She resolved to make it up to him.

When he returned, still not speaking to her, she apologized to him. Got on her knees. Begged. "Don't leave me," she had said. "Please don't ever leave me." There had been many such scenes during their brief marriage, until the final scene in which she was the one who left, back to Auntie Marie's where she was wanted. Where she would always be wanted.

THE DAY DRAGGED ON with but a few customers straggling in here or there. Tuck Michelson from down on Jericho Road stopped in for some Carnation milk because his wife was making fudge for the church bake sale. Two older Canadian ladies stopped in to use the bathroom before they hit the border. They were putting on some of the extra clothes they'd bought, Geneva knew, so that there would be no duty to pay.

By three, she was thinking of calling it a day. Closing early and crashing on the couch, watching her shows like Auntie Marie had always done. She had just about given in to the fantasy of wrapping up in a couple of old afghans and taking a nap when the buzzer rang. Outside a large tour bus was being pumped full of diesel.

Good. Would be a decent sale for the day. She'd have something to show for her efforts. It took a while for the bell on the door to ring with the bus driver's entrance. He must have filled up.

"Glad you've got diesel," he said, walking up to the counter as he dug his wallet out of snug jeans. He was an older fellow, not bad to look at. Kind eyes, thin physique. "Place in town was waiting on their delivery. Said you might have some."

"Got that and plenty more stuff surplus thanks to them."

"I hear you," the driver said. He took in her arm or lack thereof but quickly moved up to her face. Pretty. He smiled. "Times are tough all over."

Geneva blushed at his smile. Had been a long time—since back before her accident—that anyone looked at her like that. She wasn't sure she liked being appraised and appreciated anymore. She was imperfect, unlovable. A burr, a burr, stuck to you that you couldn't get off. Not something you actually sought out and attached to yourself. She dropped her eyes to the register and ran his credit card through the machine.

"Where are you headed?" she asked as the credit machine whirred out tape.

"Montreal," he said. "Charter church bus out of Plattsburgh. Got some pilgrims on the bus."

"Oh yeah?" Geneva pictured Thanksgiving dinner. Black dresses. White bonnets. A scarlet letter.

"On their way to St. Joseph's Oratory," he said, handing her the slip.

"Looking for a miracle?" Geneva asked. She had heard the story many times from Auntie Marie of how her father had prayed for help on the steps of the church during the Great Depression. How just the next day, he'd been offered the job cutting timber that led him across the border and to this store. Geneva pictured him on the stone steps—crouched, perhaps kneeling, hat in hand, snowflakes drifting down, coating his black hair in white. He may have cried as he prayed. He may have whispered more than a prayer, but a plea. And his prayer had been answered. She had planned to take Auntie

Marie up there to pray for healing, for Brother Andre had healed many—they said the crutches of those he laid hands on lined the huge stone walls. But the two of them had never made it. Auntie Marie always had an excuse—too tired, too busy, too this or too that. There had been no miracle.

Before the bus pulled away, two people got off and came to the store: a man and a woman. Later she would not be able to recall anything about the man other than his voice translating what the woman said. The woman was slight, her black hair slicked back into a tight bun, her dark eyes round and fearless. They approached and stood before Geneva, whose hips were pushed up against the edge of the counter.

The woman handed Geneva a flyer with information about their pilgrimage. "We thought we might be stranded here. She wants to thank you for having gas," the man said. Geneva nodded. The woman reached both hands out and grabbed Geneva's shoulders, said something in another language. "It's your soul," the man said. "It's that you have great longing." The woman pulled Geneva forward and kissed her once on each cheek and they left.

Geneva wanted certain things. She wanted her arm back. She wanted Cheri to stay put. She wanted not to lose the store, but there was not much else. A person didn't need much more than home and family. Geneva had always been satisfied with just that—at least until Clint screwed it all up by having an affair with the high school basketball coach's wife—the first in a string of unfortunate dalliances. He was a good looking, charming man. Few, she felt, were immune to his flirtations. At first, Geneva had taught herself to ignore Clint's indiscretions—so deep was her fear of being left alone and also so deep was her fear of being wrong about him. Of admitting that she never should have married him in the first place. She had insisted to everyone who'd listen that he was a good man. But she had been stupid. Of course she had been.

She sat on the couch with her back to the window and the dying rays of the day's sunlight and turned the flyer over in her hands.

She thought of Renee's card, now safely tucked beneath Geneva's mattress. Renee and Marie weren't even real sisters anyway. Marie from the first marriage and Renee from the second, not long after Marie's mother died and their father married Renee's much younger mother. After that second marriage, Marie came home from the convent to care for her young sister when Renee's own mother got sick. And when both parents died, Marie cared for Renee and the store alone. After a lifetime of taking care of everyone else it was no wonder Marie never married, never had children of her own. She didn't want for much.

Renee wanted something, though. Geneva figured she wanted to come back and see if Auntie Marie had any money for her. And Cheri? She just wanted to leave and sometimes Geneva wondered if she just shouldn't let her go. Their wants and desires were clear to Geneva. Always had been. But her own and Auntie Marie's were different, below the surface, unavailable. Maybe she and Auntie Marie didn't think they deserved to want. Maybe they believed that God would provide all.

Geneva took up the pen and turned the flyer over to its blank side on the table next to her and wrote. She told Renee that Marie was dead. She told Renee that there was nothing left there for her, that she and Cheri were taking care of it all. She said, "If you like, we have some money saved up and would be happy to buy out your portion of the store from you so that you would be free and clear and never have to worry about coming back here ever again." But Geneva had lied. There was no money saved to pay off Renee. If she chose, she could come up north and move right in with them. They were all partners in the business. She prayed for some divine intervention—to win the lottery or to find a bag of money by the side of the road so that Renee might stay away forever.

Geneva would get the letter in the next day's post and hope it arrived in time to stop Renee from traveling north. She had signed the note, "Geneva, Marie's own daughter," but she wasn't sure why she felt the need to say she was Marie's daughter. No one had ever referred to her that way, not even Marie.

She was a simple burr, clinging, hoping to get by unnoticed.

5

GENEVA WAS AT THE STOVE stirring something that smelled familiar when Cheri woke up from an afternoon nap and came into the kitchen. She'd been out late the night before, at the bar, talking to Seany the bartender, sharing her smokes with some guy named Bill or Mike or Jeff, looking like a puffy high-school version of himself that she barely remembered. He might have played basketball. Might have been one of the guys who cornered her behind the bus ramp that one time and called her a dyke and told her to suck their dicks to prove she wasn't. She'd said, sure, she'd suck it, but when one of them unzipped and pulled it out for her, she'd pulled as hard as she could and twisted the thing until it beat in her hand like a heart.

They called her crazy after that. Left her alone.

This guy had no idea who she was now. He just knew he could get whatever he wanted from her. And she let him know that he could when he drove her home.

Cheri leaned over the pot and breathed in. "*Tourtière*," Geneva said. "Auntie Marie's recipe." It was the meat pie her aunt made every Christmas. Cheri realized that the smell was Christmas to her—warm, spicy. Nothing since she'd left home had reminded her of that. She could almost feel her aunt in the room with them.

And then she *could* feel her aunt, her disquiet, her disgust. Her aunt knew what she was doing with her days and nights and did not approve. Her aunt wanted Geneva and her to be as they had been before when they were children. But her aunt did not understand why that could not and would not happen. The way they had been was dead.

Cheri grabbed her jacket from the hook and pawed through the wicker basket of mittens to find a matching pair.

"Where're you going?" Geneva asked.

"Out," Cheri told her as she walked out the door, leaving behind the smell of Christmas. The sky was looking fierce but she could make it to town in an hour or so, plenty of time before any storm set in.

At first the night sky spread out before Terry Plunker like someone had spilled a cool bucket of water on a smooth black floor. The water beaded. Turned to beads, illuminated from within. The black of the floor was dense, impenetrable, immense. The beads were stars and the black floor was the sky. Beads, and stars, and water, and black, black sky. But as he got closer to the store, the clouds took over and the sky became a heavy gray pillow above him, waiting to smother and weigh him down.

The dirt road he drove on was bumpy, in need of grading, but it was too cold for grading now that the winter freeze had set in. The ground was petrified until spring. It was a punishing ground, hard to the touch if you ran your fingers over the dimples of the bare earth. And the cold was enormous, as vast as the sky and everything that lay beyond the sky. Infinity.

But he liked the cold and missed it when it was gone and the ground became soft and gave way again. The brisk air brought quiet that was otherwise taken up by the sound of chainsaws and tractors and diesel engines and geese edging south and songbirds looking for mates and peepers pushing their voices out of the ooze. In the cold, all you could hear was your own feet crunching the ground. All you could hear was your own white air breathing out of you. Once in a great while if you were awake in the middle of a still winter night, you might hear an owl in the distance, out hunting for prey too camouflaged for the human eye.

He was on the tarmac again and had a mile and a quarter to go when the rain started, pecking first softly at his neck and then faster and tighter like the sharp-toothed bites of a weasel on the sides of his face. He would not make it to the store and then back home without getting soaked through, but his need of beer and smokes outweighed any desire for the comfort of dry clothes.

He hoped his woman kept the fire going back home, kept herself warm. She often forgot creature comforts like warmth and food and he would come home to find her sitting in the old rocking chair, staring out the window with no coals in the stove. When he asked her what she was doing, she said, *Thinking*. And when he asked her what she was thinking about, she said, *I don't know*. And it seemed that she really did not know what she was thinking and so he had given up trying to figure out what she thought about during those staring times. Didn't matter to him whether she thought or not, really. She was good company, soft and warm in bed at night. Always willing to let him relieve himself of his manly pressure when he climbed beneath the pile of afghans and old quilts and found her sloping back turned to him. He didn't even have to turn her over, as she let him poke himself in from behind, get his business done. She was good, his woman.

The rain picked up and glazed his hands as they held the handlebars steady. He was almost there. He could see the outline of the building, lights inside and out flickering on and off and on and then off for good. Power was out, but no matter. Didn't need power to buy beer.

He thought of his woman again. She would be cold in the dark with no light, no fire. No warmth. When he got home, he hoped to find her in bed already—the soft white part of her neck exposed so that he could touch it with his icy fingers and make her flinch so that he knew she was still alive.

IRIS COULD NOT REMEMBER a time when she was not closed up as she was, quiet and within herself. There must have been a time when she was otherwise. Sometimes the light cut through her and she felt something other than nothing, but the feeling did not last long.

She preferred it when he was gone from the house and she could sit in her chair and rock and wait. She didn't know what she was waiting for exactly, but it was something important and wanted. The return of something lost. Someone lost. A child maybe.

She had lost many children. Some of them were lost to her within her womb, while others still she had given birth to only to have them taken away by the state, given to foster homes. So many children gone.

She had a beautiful little girl once and she had thought she would keep that one baby for herself, but it wasn't to be. That girl was taken away from her and given to someone else. Never seen again.

So now Iris was the worst kind of mother: a childless one. Waiting, waiting.

THE ICE STORM STARTED when a blast of Arctic air from Canada met up with a waft of warm air from the south. Instead of the snow they should have been getting, they got a half-inch or more of ice coating the trees and the ground. Cheri was off walking down the road. When Geneva had asked where she was going, Cheri had merely said, "Out," like a sullen teenager. That's what she'd become again. She knew where Cheri went, though. Geneva wasn't stupid. That girl was on her way to town, to the hotel bar and the men she found there.

Geneva knew what people were saying about Cheri in town. About how she drank over her limit. About how she was a whore opening her legs for anyone who would have her just as her mother had been a whore before her.

Geneva tended the woodstove after the power went out, opening the lower cabinets in the kitchen and bathroom in the vain hope of getting some warm air to the pipes so they wouldn't freeze. Soon the wind picked up and the heavy branches of the sugar maple closest to the house thumped and scratched against the roof. She thought of the one time she'd been to the car wash instead of washing the old truck herself, the way the heavy blankets of fabric slapped against the windshield. How it felt like she could not breathe with the weight of them against the fender.

If she had been able, she would have cut down those branches closest to the house earlier in the fall, but she couldn't do it, her arm being what it was. Hell, she couldn't even drive a car anymore. Well, she could drive, but not manual, and not if the situation was tricky and required both hands on the wheel. At her last visit, the doctor had again encouraged her to look into prosthetics but the thought of a fake arm displeased Geneva. She'd rather be how she was. Flawed, unwhole, unholy. Many people with worse afflictions than hers had overcome them. She needed to pull herself up. To rise to the occasion. In those moments of her weakness, inside her head she coached herself, *Rise, rise. You must rise. You must rise up.*

———

As Plunker's vehicle approached the store he saw a lone light flickering through the plate glass window, someone walking around inside with a candle in hand. He followed the glow of the light as it moved like a firefly. Relief. He would be able to get his beer after all and smother the tickling in his brain.

He parked his vehicle and hustled to the door, found it locked. He rattled the handle and then rapped on the glass. The woman with the candle was the one-armed one who worked there—Geneva. He had not seen her since that day. The day when he had found her by the road, injured and bleeding and begging for his help. She had been pitiful and yet her beauty shone through, even as her face paled with the blood loss. "I'm here," he said. "I'll help you." He had told her he would go for help on his ATV but she had begged him not to leave her.

"Don't let me die like this," she said. "Not like this." She never said the word, but he knew she meant alone. Don't let me die alone.

He got her on the back of his ATV as best he could and the two of them had gone not two miles before Plunker was able to flag down another vehicle, someone faster to drive her to town and safety. When a reporter from the television station in Plattsburgh came to interview him after everything was all over, she asked him why he hadn't called someone on his cell phone. "Ain't no one got one of them things here," Plunker said, he pointed to the mountains in the distance, drew his hands together in a V. "We're in a valley here. Spotty reception." Still, the reporter seemed perplexed. Clearly she had never lived without instant communication, being from the city as she was and he didn't like how she implied that he'd done anything other than the right thing by driving off with Geneva on the back of his vehicle. He had saved her life is what local folks knew. Plunker was as close to a hero as he could be and while Geneva had never thanked him, Marie had, of course. She said to him, "You did the lord's work, Terry Plunker, by saving my Geneva's life. He will reward you." And those words of hers were enough for him. He wasn't anyone special.

He knew Geneva was grateful. Seeing her face lit from below by the candle, he knew how it would soften at the sight of him. She was different, not like the other one with the crazy black hair and the pale face and the tattoos on her wrists who lived there with her. "What are them?" he'd asked that other one, the surly one, when she'd rung him his beer and cigarettes.

"Tattoos," she said, like he was too dumb to know better. She thought they were all know-nothings, that one. She'd lived in the city and now she was back to show them all how much better she was. He longed to make her cry one day and then when she was crying he would tell her, *Go ahead and cry, little girl. Your tears ain't gold.*

"I mean," he said, "what are they supposed to look like?"

"They're shackles," she said, her face flat as shale. He wanted to ask her what they meant to her. What they symbolized. But he gave up on it. Didn't need her laughing at him afterwards. He knew about symbols. About words that meant one thing and said another. He knew that a painting sometimes had another story to tell than what was obvious to the eye. Same with people—sometimes what they showed you outside was different than what they were thinking inside. Sometimes a smile actually meant, "I hate you."

Geneva was nicer. Pretty. He would have liked to have fun with her, even without the arm. In fact, the missing arm made her better—more human and approachable. She was on his level now— certainly more than she had been when she was whole. Maybe her missing arm symbolized loss, emptiness, atonement. No. He wasn't sure what it symbolized, but it was something big and meaningful.

He rattled the handle again. She started and looked in his direction. He waved and she walked toward the door. He wondered how she would open the door with the candle in her one good hand.

He pressed his face as close to the glass as he could so she saw that it was him: harmless, a regular, the man who had saved her life. He watched the candle cross the room until her face was before him lit from below by the soft flickering light. "We're closed," she said, her voice muted by the glass. "No power."

"I know it," Plunker said. "I got cash." He dug in his pocket and pulled out a twenty, plastered it on the glass so she could see it was real. She nodded and turned the lock, keeping the candle burning in the same hand, wax dripping as it tipped.

"Careful not to burn yourself," Plunker said.

"Come in," she said. The wind blew hard and wet through the open door. He moved into the room and she shut the door behind him.

"Nasty out," Plunker said and rubbed his red hands together. She nodded, impatient for him to get on with it.

He walked to the coolers, opened one, peered in. "Don't keep that cooler open too long, please," she said. "Don't know how long the power's going to be out. Not sure even NYSEG would try fixing things on a night like this."

She made Plunker nervous, so he grabbed the first six pack he could find. It was light beer—not his typical choice, but it would have to do and he had a few pounds to lose anyway. His woman took to cooking heavier meals when it got cold out—bulked them up, kept them warm, but lately the top button of his jeans had been difficult to do up. He patted his belly. He was not a vain man, typically, but he had always taken pride in his slim physique.

"Need some smokes," he said placing the beer on the counter. She pulled down a pack of Pall Malls before he even had to say which kind. His heart thunked wildly that she knew what brand he wanted. Either she could read his mind or she had been paying attention to him—his likes and dislikes, his wants, his desires. She turned to face him. Her beauty like the cold—quiet and still. He wanted to touch her face, but his hands were smudged and filthy black from the bottles he'd collected earlier in the day when the sun had been yellow in the blue sky and all he had thought about was drinking a beer and having a smoke back at home on a calm winter's evening. He had anticipated neither the ice storm nor how seeing Geneva again would make him feel.

"Here," he said, pushing the twenty across the counter to her.

"Register won't run," she said. "I'm putting it on a tab for you, Terry, and you can pay next time." No one called him Terry. Not anymore. His woman called him nothing, rarely addressed him at all. She had no name for him.

Terry. It sounded pretty coming from Geneva's mouth.

"Yup," Plunker said. "Thanks now." Embarrassed by her kindness and the thrill it induced in him, he wanted out of that store, out to the cold and the raw wind where he could think again.

"Drive safe," she called after him. "Be careful." He would. He would be safe and slow and careful the whole way home. He would be safe and slow and thinking of her. Her quiet face, her still white hand, the way his name moved from her mouth to his ear and inside his brain where it sat and reminded him that he was once another, cleaner person.

Outside the wind cut through him with pins and needles of freezing rain, but nothing could stop his growing euphoria. He felt like he was ten again and that it was that first really warm day and that he was at the abandoned quarry with his big brothers and they all wore cut off jean shorts and no shirts and bare feet. He felt like it was that first time he took three steps back and two running leaps forward and jumped off that ledge that led down, down to the green water below. He remembered how his body knifed through the cold. They said the quarry was bottomless. That it had been abandoned when they hit a vein of water and the thing filled up and never stopped filling. He thought he might never stop sinking down into the darkness.

But then his body slowed and he began kicking upwards. All the way up he followed the murky light until he had split through into sunlight. It was that sunlight he thought of on his way down the bumpy road. Not the wind, not the ice clinking down, coating the skinny branches of the trees until they bent with the weight. No other vehicles were out, but for Plunker and his thoughts. He tried to think of a reason to go back to the store but came up empty. He would head home to his woman—quiet, and empty, and thinking in the dark.

There were tinkles and clinks at the window. Children were tapping their bony fingers against the glass, seeking entry. But by the time Iris arrived at each window to open it, the children were gone. It was a horrible, cruel trick. She left the windows open. If the children wanted in, let them come in. She would feed them.

She would cook stew for dinner. Or chicken and dumplings.

In the kitchen, she found a half-empty box of Bisquick and some chicken noodle soup. This was all. It would have to do, but she would not start cooking yet. She would wait, instead, for the children to enter the home. She would listen for their small feet clipping along the floorboards. She would need to count them to see how many biscuits were required. One per child, as it should be.

She would wait and ask them, and if they did not answer, then she would know to give them two biscuits each.

GENEVA READIED HERSELF for the cold night ahead. She would sleep in the front room and tend the fire. Cheri was not home yet. Out. She was out. Where once they had their own shared language involving hand signals and made up words, now Cheri seemed to speak a dialect all her own—one that had to do with anger and resentment.

She questioned whether having Cheri back home was worth it. She had thought it would be more like when they were kids and Cheri looked up to Geneva, cherished her beauty. That was really it, when she admitted it to herself. She wanted someone to love her again. To want to be her again. She wanted a person's jealousy, covetousness, envy. She wanted to feel that she was not weak, but desirable. It was clear that Cheri wanted nothing of or from Geneva. Cheri had two good arms and had experienced life outside of the county where Geneva had spent her whole existence. Cheri was passing time, waiting until Geneva let her off the hook by saying she could do it all herself, that Cheri was free to go. The day would come soon when Cheri would go and leave her alone.

WHEN THEY WERE TWELVE, there was no "I" for either girl, but the two of them together as one "we." This was what Marie heard: we are doing this or we are doing that. While she had raised her sister Renee and been more or less mother to her, the two of them had never been as close as these two girls were—two girls who couldn't be more different from each other.

It was a Saturday and they were sitting in the front room with

Marie, who was teaching them to knit. There was a good fire in the stove and outside the last leaves of autumn kicked up the sky. She cherished these quiet times with them, when they would sit still and focus on what she had to say. When they would listen to her and not talk and stop moving and breathe in and breathe out. She had taught them how to cook, how to shoot a rifle, how to sew, how to fish, how to clean a fish and a squirrel, and how to crochet.

She had taught them how to wash dishes and cut a sandwich and bake a cake. She had taught them hospital corners and how to wash windows (with newspaper and vinegar—do not waste money with those fancy spray cleaners). "You girls need skills," she told them, "in case there's ever another Depression with no work to be found. These skills are what will get you through. Not Algebra."

Knitting came hard to Cheri, but as always Geneva picked it up quickly. The child seemed as though she were more kin to Marie than Cheri did, really. And perhaps she was. Marie saw a lot of herself as a young girl in that child. Like Geneva, she had had to bring herself up from childhood. Marie's mother sent her off young to the convent over the border—the one in Ormstown where she herself had been raised.

Marie was twelve when her mother left her behind the brick walls, within the quiet rooms. "We are no longer worthy of raising a daughter such as you. The sisters will take good care of you here, Marie." Marie had wanted to make her mother proud, but one thing which stopped her from taking that step, from giving herself up entirely to God, was this: She wanted a child of her own. It was a selfish wish. She knew this. But it was her only one. The other thing that stopped her from giving herself up was unspeakable. Marie had sinned and because of this she was unworthy of God's love.

It was at the convent she learned most of her skills—except for the hunting and fishing, which had come from her father, who had never gotten the son he wanted. She watched the two girls as they copied her motions. Watched their sideways glances, hand signals, eye twitches. Looking at these girls you'd think that Cheri must be in awe of Geneva—how beautiful she was and how quick in her brain, but Marie knew different: It was Geneva who envied Cheri, whether she admitted it to herself or not. Cheri would come and go and stick to no one. Whereas Geneva was leaden, heavy in her organs, and stuck to this place, just as Marie was. It was in their soul.

THE COALS IN THE STOVE were bright red when Geneva put more wood on, blew on them to get a flame. It was warm by the fire. She pitied anyone out on a night like this, hoped Cheri had sense enough to stay put and not try to make her way home. She thought of Terry Plunker out there on his ATV—stupid man to travel out into the storm for beer and cigarettes. He would be wet and cold out there on the road. Maybe she should have offered him a place by the fire to warm up before he left. He was the one, after all, who had saved her. That's what people said, though she knew he hadn't done any more than any other person would have. It was her adrenaline that had really kept her alive—that's what the nurse told her anyway. So she didn't owe Terry Plunker anything after all. As always, it had been up to her to take care of herself.

Something about the way Plunker looked at her stopped her from offering him a place by the fire. There was a glimmer of that old desire she was used to seeing in men's faces. But then, it meant nothing coming from someone like him who was too ignorant to realize that she was even missing an arm in the first place.

———

MARIE HAD HOPED that Geneva wouldn't be the one. She believed that Cheri would, like her mother Renee, be a young woman who attracted stray males into the store like the town cur in heat. Yet as the girls aged there was no denying that Geneva was the beauty, Cheri the dark heart. That Geneva was the fissure, and Cheri the wall.

She had been aware ever since she took Geneva in that the girl was prettier than her niece, but she also knew that sometimes pretty little girls could turn into ugly young women, as she had. This was not the case with Geneva, who grew lovelier with each year.

At fourteen, there was no denying that grown men were coming into the store specifically in hopes of seeing Geneva. Lyle Crouch, who hadn't been in the store in close to ten years, came in for a pack of cigarettes every Friday night on his way across the border even though everyone knew he'd given up smoking. But there he was on Geneva's night behind the counter, asking her for a pack of Lucky Strikes because they were up the highest; she'd have to climb on the stool. Marie had watched his eyes watch Geneva. She was no fool.

At church on Easter Sunday, Marie saw the alms collectors nearly knock each other down trying to get to their pew so they could catch a glimpse of Geneva in her new sundress—the one she'd sewn herself with Marie's supervision. It had seemed an innocent enough dress within the walls of their home, but once they were in church, Marie found she could not stop herself from glancing at Geneva's smooth shoulders, the cleft between her young breasts, the gentle slope of her calf.

In the car on the way home, Marie said, "You'll not the work the counter anymore, Geneva. Instead you'll take stock. We can do inventory at night after close and then you'll help me with the cleaning. Cheri will run register."

"I understand," Geneva said. Marie glanced into the rearview mirror to catch a glimpse of the two girls in the backseat. Geneva looked out the window, biting her lip. Cheri stared back at her, eyes full of hatred. They had taken it the wrong way, the two of them. They thought she didn't trust Geneva because she wasn't a blood relative.

She wanted to tell them this was not about kinship. It was about protection. If anything, she loved Geneva far more than she could ever love Cheri.

PLUNKER WAS NEARLY HALFWAY between his house and the store when he ran out of gas. He had been stupid. He should have filled up at the store, but he hadn't known he needed to because the gauge was broken. He couldn't have filled up anyway. You needed power to pump the gas. He was not so stupid after all. The situation was stupid and cold and wet.

The wind picked up and Plunker stuffed his hands beneath his armpits to warm them. He looked one way up the road and then back down the other. Toward home was three or so miles and back to the store was a little over two.

He was on a long stretch bordered by fields on one side and woods on the other. Way off in the distance, acres and acres away across the field, he could see lights on in the McDougalls' house—but the only way to get there from where he was would be to cross the field, which would be rutted and unmanageable on such a harsh night. He could wait for a sander to pass by but that could be hours away and the weather might turn for the worse. Best idea was to keep moving, but which way? Would take him longer to get home, but then he'd be there—safe and warm. He could be back at the store quickly, but then there was no guarantee she would let him in, though she should. And he believed that maybe she would.

He thought of her voice saying his name and saying his name. He yearned to be near her again but he was being foolish to think a woman like her would want him. Someday she would. He would take it slow and get her to know him the way he was inside his head. She would change her mind about him. She would.

He stuffed the paper bag with the beer and cigarettes under his right arm and headed in the direction of home, hands shoved deep into the pockets of his jeans. As he walked, his thoughts stayed on Geneva. That she was flawed now made her only that much more perfect in his eyes. God or something like God had led him to this moment and this ice storm and this running out of gas so that he might find these moments alone thinking of Geneva. He no longer felt the cold.

THE FIRE DIED OUT and the children never came. Their father came like wind and their mother came like ice, but there were no children. Iris left the windows open. Let them punish her if they would. She had taken worse things from worse people. She had taken it all. Let herself lie down and be rolled over and over by people. This was the way of her life.

"Where are my babies?" she asked the father wind. "What have you done with them?" The ice, she asked as well.

As always, they would not answer her.

6

RENEE THREW OUT HER CELL PHONE at the rest stop outside Jacksonville. First she took out the battery, then she bashed the phone against the pavement over and again until it shattered into pieces. Felt good to be without the thing, unfettered by the modern world, and by Rick. He liked to always be able to get in touch with her which was why she got it to begin with and turned off her regular phone.

Her plan was to stay off 95 and take the less popular U.S. Route 1 all the way up from Florida. It felt safer to move inland, as though she and the baby were less conspicuous than on the major routes, where a person driving up the coast alone with a baby might otherwise have stuck out. People might have asked questions, for instance, where's the father, and she had not yet fully worked out her story about Cree. She knew she was going to tell folks that the baby was her own, but beyond that she was unsure.

She drove a few hours each day—never more than five—and found a quiet motel for a night if the rates were low enough. She still had plenty of cash—$2,000—but she was wary of it running out too soon. She didn't want to show up at Marie's empty-handed. Soon

Cree grew restless in the car, impatient with the routine. Maybe Cree was finally feeling better, human again or perhaps even for the first time. So Renee made more frequent stops along the way than she had anticipated in order to placate Cree, who liked to be carried and liked to have her belly rubbed. The child craved affection and human touch.

At night, Renee was careful to watch the national news to make sure that no one was on the lookout for a woman and baby. A woman with a stolen baby. But she had not stolen the baby from Mittens. That woman had given the child to Rick, no questions asked. And Rick had no claim on the baby. It's not like he was the child's father; no, he was the man who planned on selling the baby for profit. With all of this in mind, Renee felt she had nothing to worry about. Regardless she thought it best to be safe. She had not gone to the police about Rick and maybe she should have. Wouldn't she have been an accessory if he had ended up selling Cree and getting caught? And some folks might still believe that she had taken a child who didn't belong to her no matter what the circumstances, even though it was obvious she was saving the child's life. Renee didn't deserve jail or persecution. She deserved a medal.

It didn't really matter if it was taking them longer to get up north than she'd planned. Just meant Marie had more time to get used to the fact that she might soon have visitors. Renee pictured her big-bosomed sister sitting in her recliner, Cree held safely in the crook of her arm. It was a homely scene. Domestic and filled with love.

A child deserved a home, a good, clean home. A child did not deserve to be living on the streets with a junkie and certainly did not deserve to be sold to the highest bidder.

Renee was doing the right thing. Might have been the best thing she had ever done in her whole life other than giving birth herself. Within this baby was her redemption. The best part was that it seemed as though they would make it to Marie's in time for Christmas.

When she was a girl, Marie would let Renee stay up late and attend Midnight Mass and let Renee sleep with her all night long as they waited to see what Santa had brought. There was always a gift for Renee but it was never quite right—like a skateboard when she was twelve and all of the other kids had them. Renee couldn't use the thing until spring when the snow melted and so it sat in the corner of her room, leaning up against or sliding down the wall and being something to trip over. Despite Marie's efforts, Christmas always made Renee feel the motherless child—she would have liked to pretend it never existed, except for the carols. She had loved the music of the season and the feeling it gave her, as though she were holy and worthy of something special.

Now the baby would be Renee's special gift to Marie. The baby would be their miracle. Amen, amen, amen.

RICK WAITED A WHOLE LONG MORNING and afternoon for them to come back home. He called Renee's cell over and over until he got to her message, then he hung up. He figured Renee had taken the baby shopping or to the park, but then a few hours turned into many hours. When he could wait no more, he went to work, taking his mother's car, as she was already shitfaced and wouldn't miss it. He had to lie to the folks at Titty's about where Renee was. Lie that she was sick, bad off with some bug or other. But he was off his game and felt as though everyone could tell he was not telling the truth. Renee's disappearance with the baby shook him up.

He was good and pissed by the time he got home, his phone not ringing once his entire shift, and knew exactly what he was going to say to her, about how she was being irresponsible for keeping the baby out for so long. She had no idea how much jail the two of them could do for having a baby who did not belong to them in their possession. And then there was the potential buyer Rick had found through one of his sources at Titty's. This dude up in Montreal was eager, practically salivating, to purchase the baby. Not to mention that he was offering Rick twenty-five thousand dollars.

But she wasn't home that night. Or the next or the next. The phone never rang, messages went unanswered. Rick moved beyond pissed into worried. It's not like he could call the police. It was bad enough that when he had to tell work that Renee was gone, he'd dealt with the suspicious looks from both management and the customers.

"I'm telling you she up and left," he said to one of the regulars. "Took off in the night."

"Don't sound like Renee," some old drunk said, like he knew anything about Renee.

He should skip town, head south, go to the Keys and forget Renee and the baby ever existed. It wasn't the first opportunity that had gone bust on him. But he didn't want to leave yet. He wanted answers and none appeared forthcoming. Plus, he had been holding out on Renee: The baby really did belong to him to do with as he saw fit. When Mittens handed the child over, she said, "I want her to be safe." And he had promised that. And not for nothing either; he was the baby's father and had the birth certificate to prove it. Whenever Mittens could not pay, she let Rick have sex with her. And out of this union, Cree was born. Of course, he never told Renee this, as they had been together as a couple when it happened.

Betrayal meant nothing. Especially to a woman who had run away with a child that no more belonged to her than the sky belonged to the moon.

———

THERE HAD BEEN NO SNOW on the last Christmas with their father. "Nothing I hate more than a green Christmas," he told them, oxygen tank following behind him as he walked the length of the store. He would not have another Christmas. Never again one with snow. They all knew that.

"I wish I could make it snow for you," Marie said. She was behind the counter, hanging lights, trying to make the place seem more festive.

"Well, you can't," he said. Renee was tempted to reach out and crank the dial on his oxygen, turning it off, depleting his supply. He should have been dying in the hospital, but he refused. Even the visiting hospice nurse had tried to coax him to do so. "Your girls can't be expected to care for you," the nurse had told him.

"They can and they will," he said in response. "They're my children and it's their duty to care for me now. It's their turn."

Renee had not felt it her duty or her turn. Perhaps it was Marie's, but not hers. He was a mean old man who had never shown love. She thought a lonely hospital bed would have suited him fine.

He peered out the window into the empty lot. They'd not sold Christmas trees that year. No one had the energy to chop them down and set them out for sale. Across the road, the yellow grasses were tossed to and fro with the wind, bending and twisting and whipping around. The frigid whirl kicked road sand from a long forgotten storm into a spiral in the lot.

Her father's eyes locked onto the motion. For a second he smiled and then stopped, frowned. She moved closer so that she could examine his face. Furrows and cross-hatches marked the skin of his cheeks, once brown with the sun, but now sallow.

"Green Christmas," he said, turning to her. "It's not right." His eyes were gone. They were gone.

RICK FILLED UP A DUFFLE BAG of his clothes and moved four lots up, back into his mother's trailer.

"You can't stay but more than a few days," his mother said. She was used to his comings and goings, his beggings and borrowings and stealings. "I need my space."

"What the hell do you need your space for, old woman?" She should have been glad to have him. Lucky that he even spoke to her anymore.

"I just do." He would give her space all right, but not until he was good and ready to do so. First he needed a plan—but a plan was hard in coming.

An impulse led Rick back to Renee's quiet trailer. Later he believed it was the universe, looking to steer him on the right path. He couldn't get out of his mind that somewhere in that trailer was a clue to where Renee was. He kicked around for a while inside. When his search turned up empty, he left. On his way down the driveway, he stopped at the mailbox on a whim. The thing was jammed with bills and flyers but he also found something else: a letter addressed to Renee. It was his only, and possibly best, clue. The universe plopped that letter right in his lap.

Rick did not give notice at Titty's. When he told his mother that he had to leave town for a few days, the old woman was so glad to see him go that she lent him her car. Along with the keys, he helped himself to whatever else he could find in her purse. Before he left town, Rick drove down to the corner where Mittens usually hung out, waiting for a john. When he couldn't find her he asked one of the other girls and was told that Mittens had OD'd. "She's passed away," said the girl, fifteen and wearing a long blond wig, shiny against her skin. Passed away—such a sweet way to say dead. He thought of Mittens, so young herself, barely sixteen when he first met her and not yet eighteen when she had the baby. There was one less worry as he left town—no one would be looking for the baby. Nobody but him. His palms sweated with anticipation of the money and what he would do with it.

Rick plotted out on the map that it would take him a good twenty-plus hours to drive all the way into the tippy top of New York State to find the town Renee had come from. He would find Renee and the baby and he would take what was rightfully his and continue on with his plan. He would get his money if he had to kill Renee.

At this point, she was less than expendable; she was already dead to him. He stopped at a gun shop in Georgia one of his buddies had told him about and bought himself a handgun and plenty of ammo. One thing was apparent; Renee was not going to give up that baby without a fight.

AT NEW YORK, Renee got off Route 1 and merged onto I-87. She headed straight north. Not long now—six or so hours and she'd be there, at Marie's. "You're going to meet your auntie," she said to Cree. On the radio there were Christmas carols. With each mile north, she felt that things might work out okay. It was the miracle season, after all, when a child was born and wise men came and animals spoke at midnight. It was the day before the day before Christmas and she was almost home.

Home. Marie's store. But the store was her home, too. She had been born and raised there alongside Marie, her half-sister. Actually, she had been raised by Marie. More than the store, Marie was home.

Renee felt a thrill that she would soon see her sister, hug her. She had been negligent not to be in touch. Negligent not to call more often, but she had avoided calling because she didn't relish the sound of disappointment in Marie's voice that Renee was not a better person.

That would all change now. Marie would love Cree and welcome Renee back into the family. It was the season of miracles. "Blue Christmas" came on the radio—Marie's favorite carol. Renee sang along.

It was Christmastime and Marie was busy getting her food prepared. Could have used the help of the girls but they were off sulking over some teenage nonsense and who needed them hanging about spoiling her mood. "Blue Christmas" was on the radio and Marie was putting together the *tourtière*—her mother's recipe which used three kinds of ground meat: veal, pork, beef. Special ingredients: poultry seasoning and cinnamon. She had tried to teach Renee how to make it when she was a girl, but Renee had no interest. "I like the way it tastes when you make it," she said to hide her laziness. Never mind, Marie would pass this tradition on to Cheri and Geneva someday.

It had been years since Renee had been home for Christmas, but this year she had sent Marie a card in advance saying that she got the time off work and would be there. It was to be a surprise for Cheri, though Marie did wonder how the girl would take it. She'd grown not to expect much from her mother.

Though her sister infuriated her and she couldn't understand her motivations, Marie had to admit she was looking forward to the visit. Renee was always full of life and stories—she brought sunshine to the rooms of the house that hadn't been there since she'd left. Marie missed her. The *tourtière*, then, was made with special care for her sister's homecoming.

You couldn't very well taste the meat as it simmered on the stove—it was raw, dangerous. So she judged whether it needed more seasoning or not by smell. She added a dash more cinnamon as the phone rang. Even before she answered it, Marie knew it would be Renee.

"They need me at work," Renee said. "I had to cancel my ticket."

Marie cradled the phone between her shoulder and ear and stirred the meat in the pot. Her sister would not be home for Christmas.

PAST ALBANY, the rain began—the farther north she headed, the more mindfully she had to drive as the storm turned from sleet to freezing rain, the roads greasy and treacherous. By the time she pulled off in Plattsburgh, she'd been on 87 for nine hours instead of six. Her eyes were blurry, her mouth dry, and her hands ached from gripping the wheel. Cree was in need of some food and a diaper change. They found a HoJos and took their time eating and getting cleaned up.

She wanted Cree to look perfect for Marie—clean and fresh-faced. A round-cheeked, happy baby. Renee scrubbed her good in the bathroom and hummed Christmas carols. Back in the dining room, she paid the bill and left a good tip.

Outside the rain had tapered off completely. The world sparkled. Even the commercial strip that ran through this part of town gleamed in its neon and fluorescent decadence. She squeezed Cree tight to her hip and kissed the baby's cheek. "It's going to be the best Christmas ever," she said, "and it should be because it's your first one."

Less than an hour and they'd be there. Less than one hour and they'd be home.

———

THE ROADS WERE DARK out here, empty. Rick had never liked the woods. His grandfather in Georgia had taken him camping once. The only memories Rick held from that trip were of being cold and scared in the dark forest. The sounds of the creatures at night not drowned out even by his grandfather's snoring. You could have your woods, as far as he was concerned. Rick preferred the sunlight and the ocean and the beaches. This particular woods was something evil. Dark, black woods leading to nowhere. The heavy sky.

He flicked open his cell phone to call someone. Not his mother. No. Titty's? Hell no. He tried Renee one more time. He would leave a message. "I'm coming for you, baby," he said on the message. But the message wouldn't go through. Out of range.

None of it felt right and for an instant he thought of turning around, heading back, but Rick's intuition had not failed him so far. He kept on.

His car climbed a mountain. It felt like the tallest one he had ever been on. It felt like what he imagined the Alps were like or the Rockies. He would visit those mountains one day to know for sure. Perhaps he would take some of the twenty-five thousand dollars and buy some plane tickets. A nice suitcase and a suit to put in it.

He felt he would never stop ascending. He couldn't even explore the moment of ear-popping sensation because he was so keen on getting where he was going. He needed to find Renee and the baby and he needed a drink and he needed to get high. First. He needed to get high first.

He wondered if he was still alive or if he had died and this was his hell. Or his heaven. His chest tightened and he tried to suck in breath but it trapped in his throat. Then he reached the top of the mountain and started down. It was fast, steep. He kept both hands firm on the wheel, and not one dangling off his knee as he normally would. His breath would still not come, until he hit a dip and had to move quickly to catch a curve and then the air burst out of him in a wail.

He felt he would die in this place if he did not soon find Renee. He would die in these cold, dark woods and no one would ever know that he had been there at all.

When he reached the bottom of the hill and the road flattened out some, the clouds parted and a heavy moon lit his path. It was then, as the trees encroached on the road, that he could see how beautiful everything was in its coating of ice, as though all of the trees and landscape had been turned inside out and coated in silver. Perhaps this was his heaven. Perhaps it was God who led him here and getting the baby back was all part of it.

Rick was meant for something better. He knew that. Had always known it. Mittens giving him the baby was just the first phase. Now it was all about carrying through. All of this—this world, this icy world, and the trees and the mountains—it was all for him alone.

IF YOU DIDN'T KNOW what to expect on the mountain, driving it could take you by surprise. Renee knew it well—even after all these years. She remembered every twist and turn of it. She knew how, on a night like that one, the top would be covered in fog or a cloud. The top would be enshrouded, the edge of the road obscured.

And then there was the descent, where you had to plan your braking so that you didn't miss a curve and spin right off the road.

She loved it. Loved the thrill when she reached the precipice and her stomach dipped down as the descent began.

As they reached the top, she looked over her shoulder at Cree.

"Hang onto your hats, ladies and germs," she said, and then she let go and the car took over. Briefly, Renee shut off the headlights and felt herself in flight. When she turned them back on again, she saw that the dip and then the curve were approaching. She tested the brakes and let gravity pull them downward.

In thirty minutes they would be home.

7

RICK HAD TROUBLE with the steering wheel. His hands were twitching so and the leather felt alive beneath them, squirming like a snake. He had watched his grandfather kill a snake once—hacked its head off with a hatchet and yet the headless body moved. This was that snake beneath his hands, pulsing, writhing. He fought the urge to remove his hands from the wheel and wipe his sweaty palms on his jeans. He had to hold steady.

He needed something to cut through, something to pierce his anxiety, and bring him back to a state of unfeeling. His legs twitched mercilessly and sweat plastered his shirt to his chest, smothering like a poultice. He had left Florida abruptly; he had left high. But his supply was gone now, and his need was like a child that wanted diapering and bottles and constant checking up on and he had forgotten it, taken its quiet for granted, errant father that he was. If he could get his hands on some valium, he might be able to quell the urge. Hell, even a drink would help at this point. He had some cough syrup but he was saving it for when it was absolutely necessary.

The sky had cleared up considerably since the storm passed, but there was no light other than the moon. Every house he passed was dark. He might have been the last person alive and shivering in his skin, partly from the cold and the want, but mostly from the fear that was creeping up from his ankles like icy water, tensing and tightening the skin. Even his blood itched, clawing, until the hairs on his arms were like razors.

The corners of his eyes constricted and he cleared his throat. He hadn't been so close to tears since he was a small child. Crying simply wasn't tolerated in his household, not that his mother was around much to care.

He squinted his eyes and pinched his nose, but the feeling would not go away. It sat on his chest like the weight of a cat, not purring, but waiting to pounce. He thought of the last time he'd seen his father, the last time he visited him in jail before the old man died. How his dad sat before him in his orange jumpsuit. He'd aged—his skin no longer taut, but papery and creased and his eyes, pale and watery. Rick thought his father might cry then. He was no better than a woman or a small child and Rick was angry at the old man for breaking down, for not being strong enough to pull through. It was only jail. His dad had been in and out of it before plenty.

"You make me sick," were Rick's last words to his father before he left that jail for good. He didn't know that his father had only a few days of life left after that. Didn't know that he would die mysteriously in the night alone in his cell. The official word was coronary, but Rick always felt otherwise, felt some foul play had been at hand. Not that it mattered. Nothing he could do about it anyway.

He felt his father in the car with him then, sitting shotgun as he drove through this ghost world. His father's hands were clasped together between his thighs, almost in prayer, or perhaps in the pose of a man begging for mercy.

Rick knew one thing for sure: There was no mercy in this life.

He noticed some lights flickering here or there in one of the main buildings on the four corners. He parked the car and got out. As he approached he could see that his luck was holding. He knew a barroom when he saw one, whether the neon beer signs were lit or not.

A few people eyed him when he entered the smoky bar before turning back to their conversations. He found an empty seat on the corner closest to the door, and the draft that came with it, and sat down. On his right side was a young woman, tricked out in Goth gear, surely out of place in this town. On his left, a young guy in a plaid shirt and jeans, laughing with his buddies. Down towards the end of the bar, near the bathroom, he saw a young guy in a backwards baseball cap. The guy caught his eye and nodded. Rick would need him later on. But for now he would settle for a drink.

"Not even supposed to be serving with the power off like this," the bartender said.

"My lips are sealed," Rick said, his left leg jigging up and down. "Give me a Beam. Straight up." The drink went down quick and Rick got another one which he sipped. He couldn't remember the last time he'd eaten and the booze was going to his head, but not so much so that he forgot his need.

The girl next to him swiveled her seat some so that she could face him. She propped her elbow up on the bar. "What are you so scared of?" she asked. Her eye makeup was smeared and crusty, but she wasn't bad looking. On her wrists were tattooed shackles. He reached a finger out and traced the ink. He expected her to flinch or smile but she sat unmoving and staring at him.

"I'm not scared," Rick said. "Tired is what I am." He rubbed a hand over his jaw, felt the coarseness of the stubble there.

"You look like death is chasing you," she said, "and I know it when I see it." She poked her finger hard in his direction but he smiled, his eyes watering up again. He knew what she saw. He had seen it before. But Rick was not going to die on this night or any time soon. He had work to do, a destiny to fulfill. He lifted his glass in salute to her and drank it in one shaky swallow.

He turned and nodded to backward baseball cap guy. Then he got up and went to the bathroom. Soon there was a knock on the door, and the guy entered. They finished their business quickly. Rick gave the dude a blowjob and twenty dollars but all he'd gotten in return was some hash. It would not do. With the alcohol it would barely make a dent in the infant need, pawing at him, wailing for attention. He had lifted the guy up by his throat and held him against the wall until his face bloomed red.

"Give me back my $20," Rick said and then dropped him on the ground where he resembled the pile of shit that he was. The guy handed him back his money and Rick was out of there.

He twitched his way through the barroom certain that everyone could see his need hanging over him. His need picked at his scalp and so he itched and itched it until his fingers went numb. The only thing that would make it better would be to find Renee and the baby. The baby was the answer—his salvation. The baby would bring him one step closer. One more step.

CLOUDS PRESSED IN and snow began to fall as Renee approached. The store looked smaller, more ramshackle than Renee remembered it. In her mind, it had been vast and white and gleaming, but here it was before her with peeling paint and gutters stuffed full of leaves. Remembering how dearly she wished to escape this place when she was younger, she wondered whether she made the wrong choice in running right back to it now when she needed help more than ever.

She had been sixteen when she got pregnant with Cheri. It had taken her months to realize what was wrong with her. At first, because of the exhaustion, she thought it was mono, so she spent many afternoons in the nurse's office, lying in the darkened back room on a cot with a dampened paper towel on her forehead, complaining of a non-existent migraine. The room had smelled of a mixture of rubber and witch hazel and though it was stuffy she found it comforting, like a grave.

But then she began to grow and as she did she wore her clothes baggier and baggier—old sweaters of her father's over jeans she kept unbuttoned. It wasn't long before she felt the movement of the baby inside her—so thrilling and terrifying to have proof of this life. First there was a wriggle down low, but as the baby grew the squirms became deeper and more powerful. Undeniable.

The one place she could not hide was in gym class. She could claim illness only so many times before she was forced to participate or risk having a notice sent home to Marie. She noticed the other girls looking at her as she changed out of her gym clothes, laughing in small groups, whispering behind their hands. But no one said anything. Not until Ms. Lyons, the gym teacher, cornered her when she was coming out of the shower and said, "You know you need to see a doctor, right?"

Renee wrapped her towel around her torso, looked down at her feet, red from the stinging water. She had heard hot water could bring on a miscarriage. She had never missed a shower or a bath since hearing that.

"It's not healthy for you or the baby if you don't." The only doctor available to her without getting Marie involved was the one at the clinic and there was no way Renee was going to him. The one and only time was for her first gynecological exam. There had been no nurse in the room while the doctor's hands roamed her body. He ran his hands down her calves, up her thighs. He examined her young breasts in great detail. He told her he was making sure everything was in order, but she couldn't help but feel that he was doing something wrong.

"I'm not how you think I am," Renee said to the gym teacher and then she got dressed, went to her locker, and cleaned out all of her personal items and left school. She walked the five miles home and never went back to school again. Four months later she gave birth to Cheri. Several years later she left town.

The store stood for so much back then—her oppression, her shame, her lost parents. It seemed a place heavy with grief. Had there been good times, she had pushed them down and away so she would not feel longing. But then there was the hope of Marie and how she would make everything okay for Renee now. How she would keep them safe.

Renee got out of the car cautiously so as to not slip on the ice and plucked the baby out of the back seat. From the trunk she withdrew two small bags—enough to get them through the night—and stepped forward. A sander blasted past, chains jangling, lights illuminating the parking lot briefly so that Renee could see a path forward.

She fully expected the door to be locked and for her to have to use the hidden key stuck on a magnet up under the bug zapper, but instead she found the door ajar. Not like Marie to leave things this way. Must have been the storm blew it open. Renee shivered against the cold and pushed her way in. Her plan was to wait in the living room until morning so as not to startle Marie. She and Cree would sleep on the couch. It would be nice, cozy. The next day maybe they'd bake cookies and pies together. The baby squirmed, and whimpered. Renee found a pacifier and stuffed it in her mouth.

The store's interior looked the same as always—orderly, dust free. She breathed in and smelled the familiar—mothballs, Lysol, and dusty Necco wafers. Home. She smiled thinking of her days here as a child, how she had learned to run the register and bag groceries. She imagined Cree would learn these same things and they would serve her well. She would never be without purpose.

She pushed open the door to the house expecting the sharp and pleasant odor of Marie's Christmas tree—always a blue spruce cut from the patch planted by their father out back. Instead all she smelled was wood smoke and damp clothing. A fire burned in the stove and all was quiet.

BACK AT HIS SEAT, he finished up another drink and bought one for the woman next to him while he settled his tab. "Merry Christmas," he said to her, when she nodded her thanks.

"Is it Christmas?" she asked. He wasn't actually sure so he left the question unanswered.

Her eyes were like his father's had been that last time he'd seen him. Her eyes could see that death was close by. Her eyes had given up her soul. He felt them burning through his clothing, marking him. She could see right through as though he were already dead.

"You need a ride?" he asked her.

"Yeah," she said and slid off her stool. "Let's go."

WHEN PLUNKER GOT HOME, he found his woman in front of a cold fire. He wanted to curse her for being so foolish but stopped himself. She didn't mean any harm. She never did. "You go on to bed and get warmed up beneath the covers," he told her, and then he closed the windows and built the fire up until the room was warm. He hung his wet clothes from pegs and over the backs of chairs and settled himself down beneath an old cover, beer in hand. He couldn't get his mind off Geneva.

From the way their eyes followed her, he knew that most of the men in town found Geneva beautiful, and so did he, but also wary, like a caged bitch not wanting to be messed with anymore. She was also careful to cover up her deformity, lest anyone notice it. He knew what that felt like, to always hide some part of yourself away. To live knowing that you would never be whole the way others were. He kept his mind hid up tight in his head. No one would ever know how far down his thoughts went or how far out into the universe and beyond and beyond that.

The difference was that he had been this way since birth and she was only getting to know what it felt like. He was lucky, almost, to not ever have been otherwise formed and then turn the way he was. He only knew this one, this perfect, way to be.

He thought of when she turned her back to him earlier and for a moment, from the angle where he stood, she appeared normal—a two-armed woman. It was when she faced him that you knew she was not right. She didn't seem to understand the strength of her difference. That her deformity did not detract from her strength. Rather, it made her superhuman.

He thought of his mother when he was a small boy telling him not to expect too much from the world. Telling him that this life was one of disappointment. "People are cold," his mother had said. "People ain't nothing but cold assholes." And for most of his life he had agreed with her. But he had found some moments of warmth.

He bent forward and opened the grate, stirred up the coals and put another log on. Outside the wind beat punches against the clapboards and snow pushed against the windows. He thought of Geneva and how she must look while she was sleeping. He hoped she was dreaming of the two of them walking out into the crystalline world, hand in hand, walking over the ice as smoothly as Jesus did when he walked on the water.

When the storm let up, as it would do eventually, he would leave this warm place and make his way back to her. He would let her know that his heart belonged to her alone.

8

"MARIE? WHERE ARE YOU?" Geneva heard the voice, familiar, out in the main room, moving up the hall, yanking open the door to Auntie Marie's room. It would be dark in there. They'd closed it up good, left it clean as she'd have wanted it. "Marie…" the voice came toward the door to Cheri's room where Geneva sat on the unmade bed, waiting for Cheri to return. The voice had gone from screechy and frantic to mournful, understanding, grasping, maybe, that there was no longer a Marie to find.

Geneva felt a cough stir in her throat and fought to stifle it but could not. The door opened then and Renee stood with a baby on her hip. "Where's Marie?" she said.

Geneva recognized Renee easy. She hadn't changed much—not her looks and not her demanding and selfish attitude.

Renee stepped closer. "What's going on here? Where's my sister?"

"Marie's dead. Cancer. She wanted you to be here but we couldn't find you. I sent you a letter. Didn't you get it?"

Renee crumpled to the floor and sat there sobbing on the rug, holding the wailing baby. Geneva stepped over her and walked out of the room. She needed air. She needed a drink. She left the flashlight behind in Cheri's room, burning down its battery. The hallway was dark but she had traveled it so many times that she knew exactly where each step would take her.

EVERYTHING REDUCED down to the size of a pinprick—a pinprick of light, sucking all of the air out of Renee, removing all hope. Her body lost itself in chills and sobs. Cree rested against her, sniffling.

Marie was dead and there was no one to protect them now. No one. That girl was a liar, a fake, a cheater. There had been no word of her sister's passing. Renee had been foolish not to call first, not to make sure everything was okay. She had been foolish to believe that all she had to do was get back to Marie and everything would work out.

Renee lowered herself onto the bed and maneuvered until she and Cree were snuggled in tight next to the wall.

CHERI'S UNDERWEAR AND JEANS were down around one of her ankles; the other ankle was entirely bare and unfettered as she straddled the man in the car. Her arms were out of her t-shirt and her breasts pushed out of her bra. He was half lying down on the seat and she could see her reflection in the snowy window above his head.

She looked different to herself, wavy. She looked pretty, pale. A ghost of the bad Cheri—this one was good. She watched her two arms. She watched her hands gripping the man's shoulders, pushing him, pulling him, whatever. She didn't want to let go. Then her reflection did not look like her, but like Geneva, beautiful and cold and judgmental. In fact, judging her. Judging Cheri for being with this man. She shut her eyes and beat her body harder against him.

They were being quiet. It was unspoken that they would be. It was also unspoken that it was okay to do this thing together.

Quiet. Moving against each other. She opened her eyes and saw Geneva in the reflection again. Opened her mouth. There was sound at the back of her throat ready to come out. Then she saw the man's hand in the reflection covering her mouth. "Shhhh," he said. "Quiet." She stuck the tip of her tongue out and tickled the firm skin of his palm.

Later, in the moving car, Cheri believed her mother was the driver and she was the passenger. It was Christmas Eve and they were on their way to church to meet Auntie Marie. The music. Christmas carols on the radio. The sides of the roads were lined in tall, dark pine trees dressed in white snow.

It was so cold that their feet had crunched on the way out to the car. "Listen to that," her mother said. "That means the earth is freezing up good. Don't forget that sound when you're grown up and moved away from here." The snow squeaked beneath her boots. She would not forget.

To Mass they were headed. To Midnight Mass. It would be their last Christmas together.

I hate you, she said to her mother now—but then she had been quiet. She had watched and listened and let herself have these final moments.

Her mother swerved the car on purpose, laughed, and said, "That'll wake you up." Her mother always played these games in the car, where she would shut off the lights at night and drive on into the darkness until Cheri finally freaked out and screamed for the lights to go back on; her mother would comply reluctantly. "You don't really know you're alive until you think you're going to be dead. Otherwise you might just as well sleep your life away. Is that what you want?" her mother would ask and tap a finger on her forehead. "Wake up, little girl. Wake up."

But now they were back on the road, out of the swerve. It was time for her mother to go. She wanted her mother not to go. To stay with her forever as they were.

"I don't want to wake up," Cheri said. "I don't want you to go. Stay here with me. Please don't go."

"I can't stay," her mother said. "You're better off without me."

"Please don't leave me," Cheri said. "Stay. Stay."

RICK HAD BEEN STUPID to take the girl with him. She'd directed him to some dark, godforsaken road, and then she'd climbed on top of him and had her way. Shortly afterward she fell asleep and he could not rouse her. He wanted her gone.

He sat in his parked car for a while, smoked a cigarette, pondered his predicament with Renee. His one sure feeling was that blood was going to be spilled before it was all said and done, though he wasn't sure whose blood it would be.

He was tired. Maybe they could work things out. Maybe they could forget about the money and live as a couple with this child as their baby. Sure, he didn't like the cold up here but maybe he could get used to it after all. In the backseat he had an old quilt of his mother's. He pulled it forward and wrapped himself in it. He needed to nap for a bit, clear his head. Let the girl freeze.

When he woke, it was near dawn. His head felt clearer and he was resolved to move forward with his initial plan. Renee was either with him or she was against him and right now she was against him. He nudged the girl but she would not rouse. She looked younger in the morning light, vulnerable. He questioned why he'd brought her. He would dump her as soon as he found the store.

He headed north, the way his directions suggested. The wind had picked up and blew snow across the road. Rick had no gloves.

His fingers felt like claws gripping the cold steering wheel. The booze had warmed him but not enough to ever get used to the temperatures.

The windshield was obscured by snow. Rick turned on the wipers. The setting moon came in and out of view as clouds pushed over it. He'd have liked to pull over and smoke another fat one and stare at the moon for a while, but there was no time.

But no. He was answering to no one but himself. He had all the time in the world. Except he didn't feel that he did. He sensed that his time was winnowing down to nothing and that he had to finish this thing up, get this baby, get his money, move on.

OUT IN THE MAIN ROOM, Geneva tended the fire, placing a few logs on the burning embers. For the first time ever, she cursed Marie for being so stubborn about treatment. She might have been saved. Might have still been there to help Geneva with this night's mess, and the mess of the bills and the back taxes. Now they would be expected to share the premises as owners.

Everything was falling apart, slipping down. As the wind picked up outside, branches splintered under the weight of the ice and fell to the hard earth. Renee was back, was home. She would want to take over. Would want answers on the state of things. Geneva dozed off and on thinking of Renee until the fire died down. As dawn approached she felt a chill up her legs and realized the chill was real and coming from the store. She got up to check things out. The sky was now light enough that she could see clearly without a candle.

The front door was wide open—pinned that way by a box which had blown into the jamb. She went to the door and kicked at the box until it was out of the way, then she set to shutting the door. Before she could get it fully closed, a car drove by and pulled into the lot.

When it passed she noted that its license plates were similar to those of the car already parked there—Renee's car. Both from Florida.

ACCORDING TO THE MAP, the road Rick was on was a straight shot to the border. There weren't many roads he could have mistaken for his destination as all along the way, the main road was bordered by large tracts of farm land and long driveways leading up to barns and houses. He found his turn and there it was: the store.

When he pulled in and parked, he saw a woman at the door, struggling to close it in the wind. At first he thought she was Renee but then he noticed she was not—this woman was younger and she had only one arm. Still, he felt for her, something. She had a hard-edged beauty he was unaccustomed to.

He waved so she'd see him there and not lock the door and then he got out. "Hey," he said. "Hey there, miss." He tried to jog across the lot to where she was but lost his footing and after regaining his balance had to walk with more care. She stood in the door waiting for him as he inched in her direction.

"Hey," he said again, feeling stupid in her presence.

"We're closed," she said.

"I'm looking for a woman," he said and then so she wouldn't think there was something wrong with him, "and a baby. A woman and a baby. Woman's named Renee. She's got my child." Her face showed nothing. Not a hint of recognition.

"You better come on in," she said.

He hesitated at the open door. It was an opportunity, he felt. He could have turned there and left and never looked back. The room he was entering was dark, unknown. There was nothing familiar except for the possibility of finding Renee, of getting his money. There was no reason to be scared. All he had to do was follow.

———

ON HER WALK THROUGH the store to the house, Geneva tried to puzzle out in her mind what was going on. He'd said that Renee had his child, meaning the baby wasn't hers. Or maybe the baby was their child together. And while he seemed friendly, there was something panicky around his edges—veiny hands shuddering by his sides, eyes widening and shortening as he spoke—as though he were a man who would stop at nothing to get what he wanted. Geneva had known her share of this sort of man. Clint such a one. He had convinced her that if she didn't marry him, no one else would ever want her. "You've got my mark on you," he had told her when she hesitated at his marriage proposal. "No other man's going to want a girl with another man's mark upon her." The proposal had come out in the open in front of the whole town as they piled out of the school after her high school graduation. She had given up thinking he would ever ask her to marry him and though she thought she wanted it more than anything, she hesitated and she wasn't sure why. She hadn't known what he meant by his mark but felt it was important that she pay attention to this warning. Later she would realize it had been a lie—something made up to make him seem more special than he was, more important. She should have gotten rid of him right then and there.

Her mind flashed to the rifle behind the counter. She wished she'd thought to move it into the house when the power went out. Once she entered the house, it would be hard for her to get back to the store if she needed it. She couldn't quite answer for herself why she thought she would need it, other than the air felt off-kilter in this man's presence. As though he should not be there.

Inside, the room was warmer than it had seemed when she left it, the woodstove keeping the temperature up. "Have a seat," Geneva said. "I'll get her."

He sat down without saying a word and she walked down the hall. She hoped that Renee and the child would be gone—slipped out a back window and escaped. Bringing them forward to him seemed wrong to her now.

Back in Cheri's bedroom, the flashlight burned on though the light was wan now, wavering. In the bed she made out the forms of the baby and Renee, asleep.

She watched them for a while. He wanted that child. Maybe if she asked him to let them sleep and wait until they woke on their own, he would. She did not want to wake them.

She would tell him no. She would tell him she would not wake them. She turned to go and do that, but there he was in the doorway, leaning on the jamb.

"They look cozy," he said. "Shame to wake them."

"Yes," Geneva said. Her stomach flipped. Maybe he was okay.

"But we have to," he said. She stood facing him. He was thin, wiry. His face was handsome, but tight and mean at the same time. She could block him, push him out the door, lock it behind her, refuse him entry.

He stood straight and reached under his shirt and pulled out a handgun. Wind beat against the window, rattling all of the panes. The baby stirred and whimpered before settling back down.

9

"You keep this fire up," Plunker scolded his woman. "I've got to collect my vehicle but I expect you to be good and warm when I get back." She nodded beneath the pile of blankets that had kept her from freezing to death in the night. He was frustrated that she would so easily let herself die if he wasn't around and frustrated that it was his responsibility to take care of her. He felt he'd been taking care of others his whole life—his mother and now this one. Women were more trouble than they were worth sometimes.

His brothers had all scattered and left him, the youngest, to take care of their mother. One had moved a few towns over and moved in with a woman and her six children. Another was in and out of jail for various indelicacies—robbery, DUI, battery. Another, the best one, had joined the military and taken part in Desert Storm. They didn't hear from him much anymore as he spent his time in the hospital mostly.

And then there was Plunker. "You're my soft one," his mother always said. "You're the one going to watch over me in my old age." But really she hadn't been so old. She'd started having her boys at fifteen and was done having them by the time she was 20. So she was only 20 years older than Plunker when she died, gasping for breath, of lung cancer. She might have been his sister.

There weren't many women Plunker knew who didn't need taking care of by a man. Except for Geneva. She didn't need taking care of. Even deformed she seemed capable of anything.

Now it was morning and even though he had barely slept the night before, Plunker was too wired to rest. Typically, making enough cash for beer and cigarettes was all that was on his mind at the start of a day, but he found that he could not stop thinking of Geneva. He felt an urgency to reclaim his vehicle, but this, too, was an excuse to see her again. She had been everywhere in his sleep. And not only the sight of her—the smell of her skin and the taste of her on his lips.

He had always liked women. Hell, he'd lost his virginity at age eleven thanks to his older brothers. They brought him to the quarry on his birthday—a hot summer's day—and there was Heffy Lefavre. Everyone knew of her reputation, though she herself was but fifteen. On the bus the boys whispered about what Heffy would do for you, would do with you. "You don't even have to pay her," his oldest brother, Burt, said. "She just does it." It's not that she wasn't right in the head, it was that she wasn't right at all. Folks said her own father and brothers had fun with her, too, and now his brothers offered Heffy up to him. Plunker had been scared, terrified, when she spread her fat thighs, but his brothers cheering him on and his desire to prove to them that he could do it won over. So he screwed her as they watched and cheered. And in her face, he saw nothing, not sadness, not anger, just nothing. She was his first.

And there had been plenty of others before Iris, some he cared for and many he didn't, but he had never felt like this about a woman before—that he would do anything for her. And he didn't even need to screw her. He wanted to be near her and watch how her one hand fiddled with her silky hair.

He was going soft, sure. No sense in thinking she would even want him nearby, but he couldn't help himself. He set out before dawn with extra mittens and a wool cap on his head to carry his gas can back to the store. It would be a long cold walk but he could make it in a couple of hours unless he hitched a ride.

He didn't know what he'd do once he got there, but maybe he'd tell her what he thought of her. Maybe she'd feel the same way.

ONCE HE LEFT, it didn't take long for the fire to die down again. Iris let it. The children had not returned to her in the night. Her vigil carried on and she did not wish to leave the safe cocoon of her blankets. She pulled them up higher around her neck until they were covering her head and then her face, with only a small open patch for breathing. Even that felt like an invasion.

He had left her alone all night, claimed the storm had gotten the better of him, but she could tell otherwise. There was another woman taking his attention.

He was leaving her, as everyone always did. In the end there is no one there to guide you or keep you warm. There is only you.

RENEE WOKE IN A ROOM both familiar and unfamiliar. It was her childhood room, where she'd spent all her school years until Cheri was born and it became the room they shared. When Cheri grew too big to share with her mother, it became her room alone and Renee slept in the sewing room. She lay still as her eyes adjusted to the light, and her brain to the voices and shapes. The first one she recognized was Cree, her baby, cooing. That is how she had come to know Cree now: her own child with whom she would never part.

And then the other young woman, the foster girl that Marie had taken in and raised, and then Rick, pale and strung out and shaky. Rick with a gun in his hand. She pulled Cree in tight and pinched her eyes shut.

CHERI WOKE UP in a car in the parking lot of the store. She was half dressed and her head was splitting down the middle, mouth dry, eyes crusty. She tried to move but the pain in her head pinned her to the seat. She needed to get in the house now and get a shot of something to get this thing under control.

She pulled on her clothes and forced herself out of the car. She bent at her waist and heaved a stomach full of bile onto the tar. She felt a bit better as she moved to the building. Cheri pulled the door tight behind her as she entered the store. She stopped behind the counter and reached up high behind the row of cigarillos to find the pint bottle she'd hidden there. She took a swig of vodka and shuddered. Took another drink, replaced the cap, and the tucked the bottle into her back pocket. She felt better already.

Inside the main room, she took off her boots and set them by the stove. She tiptoed down the hall to her room. As she entered, the electricity flickered and clicked on and the room was lit brightly from overhead. Still, Cheri felt she was not seeing things clearly. Geneva was there with some others. Cheri made a small noise in her throat and Geneva turned to her and Cheri saw fear in her face for the first time ever. There was a man there, one who looked familiar to her and there was her mother. Her mother on the bed with a baby. Cheri reached back in her pocket and pulled at the bottle. She wanted to be prepared for anything.

GENEVA'S FIRST THOUGHT was to walk away from the situation. To tell the man with the gun to do whatever he wanted. Whatever was going on between him and Renee was their business and she wanted no part of it.

She wished, again, for her rifle, not even sure what difference it would have made, but at least it would have been something to hold against a man with a gun. She felt, once again, the powerlessness of living with one arm. Had she been whole, things might have been different, but as she was not, there was no sense in fighting.

RICK HAD THOUGHT he would come in, find Renee, get the baby and be gone before anyone had a chance to raise a stink. But he hadn't thought he'd be up against all of these women, this cold, this distant place. He couldn't think clearly and his hands shook. It had been a long time since he'd used a gun—really used one. There seemed so much time and space between him and pulling the trigger.

He might need food or water. He might need to take a leak or a dump. He might need more sleep or fresh air. He was sure he needed all of these things at once as the room constricted.

He lurched in the direction of the bed, reached for Renee, the baby. "Give it to me," he said. "It's mine." He tried to rip the screaming infant from Renee's hands but as his hands made contact, he felt a crack across his skull as he was simultaneously pushed back from the bed by another woman. He spun around and soon he was falling forward, forward falling, into the torso of the one-armed woman. He landed soft against her and she managed to hold him up as he lost consciousness and was gone.

THE MAN'S EYES ROLLED BACK into his head as he fell forward and she saw their whites, up close and stained yellow, as he landed against her body. Cheri had hit him in the back of his skull with her pint bottle. Geneva's knees cracked beneath her and she struggled to keep from falling to the floor with him.

"Help me," she said, "Cheri, help me." Cheri was beside her then, easing the man to the floor. Geneva took the gun from his hand and opened the chamber. Fully loaded. She handed it to Cheri. "You keep this on him. I'm getting some rope." Cheri looked down at the revolver in her hand and back up at Geneva. "Aim the gun at him, Cheri," Geneva said. "Back up a bit, aim it, and hold it steady. Shoot him if he moves."

She could count on no one. Not one person to do exactly what she asked. Out in the store she found some clothesline and grabbed her rifle. Back in the room Geneva handed the rope to Cheri and had her hog-tie the fellow while Geneva took over the handgun.

"You want to tell us about him, Renee?" Geneva asked.

"Never seen him before," Renee said. She sat pushed up against the wall, the baby held tight against her body. Geneva gave her a look. "Don't know him," Renee said.

"Well he knows you," Geneva said. "And he's got Florida plates same as you. So."

Geneva watched Cheri lift her head quick to glimpse at her mother. Renee flinched.

"His name's Rick," Renee said. "He's my boyfriend. My ex."

"And what about that one?" Geneva said, nodding at the child. "He said he's here looking for his child."

"She's not his," Renee said fiercely. "She's mine." The baby grabbed at Renee's breast and nuzzled as if to illustrate the point. Cheri's head dropped slightly. Rick groaned. Cheri tightened the ropes.

"Well," Geneva said, pushing a pile Cheri's clothes off a cane chair in the corner and sitting down. "I suppose we can wait for him to wake up and get his story. Or we could call the troopers right now."

"No troopers," Renee said, scooting to the edge of the bed.

"You better talk then," Geneva said. "Because I'm not liking the feel of this situation."

HER MOTHER WAS IN THE ROOM with them. Her mother and a baby and a man and it was Christmas Eve or Christmas or the day after. She wasn't sure which. Cheri's head throbbed and her throat was dry and she wanted a cold drink of water and some air but she could not leave the room until she heard everything, every word her mother said.

There was something about a junkie giving the baby to Rick and Rick telling Renee to keep the baby for herself, to take care of her. "He told me to keep her," Renee said. "She has no one else." No one else. Cheri had a mother once and then she had Auntie Marie and now she had no one else.

She wanted to grab the baby from her mother and throw the thing to the ground and stomp on it until it stopped moving. She wanted to shake her mother until she was sorry. Shake her mother until she admitted she was bad and wrong and that she should never have left.

Cheri finished tying the man and moved away from him, stood with her back against the wall, feeling an ache between her legs. She vaguely recalled having sex the night before but could not recall with whom. She only remembered her own body moving.

When Renee finished talking, Geneva spoke. "Cheri," she said. "Grab that rifle." Geneva nodded to the corner where the rifle was leaning against the wall. Cheri did as she was told.

The room was silent and they all focused on the man. Waiting.

10

IRIS FELT A JILT—a hinkiness—in her chest as she tried to draw breath. There were spiders in her lungs, crawled in as she slept. She had tried to teach herself to close her lips when she was unconscious but she always woke to find them open again. One day she would try to tape them shut for this would surely keep the creatures from finding a way in.

The fire was entirely out now and it was cold in the dark room, though she did not feel it. She had not eaten in days, and the last time she had had water was the day before. She felt as though she might be able to slake her thirst. But not water. Not water.

Water was evil. It would be her undoing and had been prophesied to her the last time she was in the bug house. The doctor had told her that a man would go down to the shore and there he would betray her. She would know when the time was right to refuse his attempts at kindness and to disregard his offers of food and drink. She would know that his fire was not so much meant to warm her as it was to remind her of the fires of hell to which she would one day return.

She would take a drink of the blood of Christ, found in the kitchen cabinet and labeled Blackberry Brandy. He had put it in this vessel to trick her, but she knew otherwise. It had been written. It was scripture.

The trip to the kitchen took longer than anticipated as she stopped often to steady herself from the dizziness. When she was not looking for them, she found the bottles everywhere, but now her search proved more difficult. But there, behind a can of SpaghettiOs, she found the vessel. She took it from the shelf and held it up to the light.

Take this all of you and drink from it.

Iris sat and drank the liquid. It was firey and sweet like summer's bright green leaves, the way one would hope Jesus would taste. *Amen.*

CHERI DIDN'T REALIZE how deep the silence was between them until her mother spoke. "How you been?" Renee said. The question seemed impossible to answer so she said nothing. "You look good," Renee said. "You're grown. Tall." Cheri caught her mother looking her up and down, taking in the length of her legs, tattoos laced around her wrists, navel piercing poking out from beneath her shirt. She wished she had more clothes on. A suit of armor.

"That's what happens. Kids grow up," Cheri said.

Renee had fixed a bottle for the baby and soon the baby had fallen asleep again. Renee put her gently on the bed, stood and stretched. "Can I bum one of these?" she pointed to the cigarettes on Cheri's nightstand.

"Suit yourself," Cheri said. She watched as her mother took not one but two cigarettes out of the pack, lit them both and brought one to Cheri.

"Here," she said, holding the cigarette out to Cheri. "Peace."

Cheri took the cigarette. Peace would take much more than a lit smoke. Seeing her mother up close and full on now, Cheri took the opportunity to really look at her. She was still beautiful but now there were lines around her eyes and mouth. She had aged, though it was hard to tell from far away. Her mother's skin was tanned turkey brown, whereas Cheri's was as pale as the moon.

She watched as her mother nudged the man with her toe and bent down over him. She touched two fingers to his neck. "When did Marie pass on?" she asked without looking in Cheri's direction.

"Few months ago," Cheri said. "I guess." Renee stood and faced her, took a drag of the cigarette, winced, and exhaled. "She had her own morphine drip," Cheri said.

"Did you get her a nice stone?"

"A cross," Cheri said. "Like she wanted. She's next to your dad."

"Your grandfather. That's good," Renee said. She walked to the empty beer can on Cheri's nightstand and dropped the cigarette butt inside it. It hissed and was out. Renee bent and stroked the baby's head. Cheri lifted the gun and aimed it at her mother's back. It would be so easy to pull the trigger.

The baby stirred and her mother stood up straight, stepped back, without turning around. She stopped moving and Cheri felt she must know the gun was on her, that she was close to death. It felt wrong then to even think that she might fire the gun and let a bullet enter her mother's flesh. She turned the gun back on the stranger lying tied on the floor.

WHEN THERE WERE BUT A FEW sips of liquid left in the vessel, Iris replaced it where she had found it. She was warm now, hot even. She stripped off the blankets and let them fall around her on the chair.

The bands of her sweater were tight around her neck and wrists. She pulled it over her head and dropped it to the floor. It wasn't enough. All of her clothes must go and then when she was unfettered she must cleanse herself. Remove all trace of this life she had been pretending to live beside the man who would betray her.

THEY WAITED UNTIL CLOSE to nine before the man started to rouse. "Get him some water," Geneva said to Renee. "Fill one of the plastic cups out there."

She wanted Renee out of the room when he first spoke. Wanted his honest reactions.

"Help," he croaked. "I can't move. Help me."

"You're fine," Geneva said, looking him in the eye as his head turned in her direction. "You remember where you are?"

"Hell," the man said, "except it's cold."

Geneva laughed. "Damn right," she said. "This is the north country. Why'd you come up here if you can't take the cold?"

"To get my baby," he said.

"And what about Renee?"

"She's the one who stole my baby." He coughed and winced. "What're you doing here?" he said when he noticed Cheri.

"I live here," Cheri said.

The man laughed and shook his head. "It figures."

"You can probably cut his legs loose from the arms," Geneva said to Cheri. "Let him sit up. Get the circulation going." Cheri did as she was told and helped the man move into a seated position.

"Thanks," he said and Geneva nodded.

"Why'd she steal the baby?" Geneva asked.

"Because she's nuts," Rick said, straining against his ropes. "She's insane." Geneva caught Cheri's quick glance at her.

Renee stood in the door with the cup of water in her shaking hand. "People need to watch what they believe when it comes to you," she said. "Tell them the truth, Rick. Tell them about Mittens."

"Mittens is dead," Rick said, "and that baby is mine. And that's the truth, the whole truth, and nothing but the truth."

"How'd you figure that?" Renee said. "She might as well be mine as yours."

"I'm her daddy," Rick said.

"Liar," Renee said.

"You can believe what you want," Rick said. "But I've got the birth certificate to prove it." Renee dropped the cup of water and everyone watched as the spill covered the floor, edging up to the rug in the center of the room.

"He only wants money," Renee pleaded with Cheri and Geneva, "and doesn't care about this child. He's going to sell her. He has someone wants to buy her. This baby."

"Told you she was crazy," Rick said. "Who would sell a baby?"

"Believe me," Renee said. "Whether he's got a birth certificate or not, this baby is mine." Cheri ran from the room. They heard her slam the bathroom door, and then the sound of her vomit hitting the toilet bowl.

"Crazy," Rick said, shaking his head, laughing. "You going to untie me or what? Because where I come from this is called criminal confinement and it means going to jail for a good long time."

GENEVA HAD LISTENED carefully to what Renee said and watched her face for any twitches or signs of lying. She was fairly certain Renee was most likely telling the truth.

Geneva startled when the gas buzzer rang, forgetting all about the fact that they might have customers. "You two stay here and watch him," she said to Cheri and Renee. Out front she found Plunker, waiting with a gas can. She turned on the pumps and watched him from the window. As she watched him in the morning light a plan began to form in the corner of her mind. Then the plan blossomed and pushed forward until she could not ignore it.

THE QUARRY WAS BACK a mile or so off an abandoned road, first used by the quarry workers and then taken over by loggers. Past where the road split there were a few more miles to the border. During Prohibition, it had been frequented by rum runners. There were one or two abandoned cars along the route, if a person knew where to look for them. Their rusty hulks, inert amongst the shady trees, now were homes to squirrels and other critters. The border patrol were aware of the road, had been for years, but since only locals knew of it, they rarely spent government time worrying over it. Folks nowadays were soft and only a fool would ever think to use this wild and dangerous route as a way across the border. It was too easy to wander off the trail and find yourself deep within the unforgiving woods.

It hadn't been too cold of an autumn and winter had barely kicked in and so Plunker figured the ice augur would serve him well for the task at hand. He squatted at the edge of the quarry and looked across to the cliffs. He'd only been out this way once or twice in the winter. It was a summer place, meant for swimming and horsing around. And now here he was, wondering where to start drilling the damn hole.

Geneva had asked him to do it. "I'll pay you," she said. "You need to be quick, though."

He said sure he'd do it, but he'd take no money from her after all was said and done. It was a gift he wanted to give her. A Christmas present, he would tell her.

She'd asked him to get out to the old quarry and make a nice-sized hole for her in the ice. "Out in the middle," she said. "Where the water is good and deep." And when he asked her how big around the hole should be she said, "It should be big enough for an adult person to fit through."

"You going for a swim or what?" Plunker joked.

"Keep quiet," Geneva answered. "Don't say a word about it." She looked so pretty then, her cheeks hot and red, that he wouldn't have told Jesus if he'd been standing in front of him with holes in his hands and feet. She gave him an extra can of gas for the trip there and back. It was a good five miles from the store and then another mile or so bushwhacking on the overgrown road.

The day was sunny and brisk, wind tinkling through the ice-covered branches. Christmas Eve. Plunker heard chainsaws coming from all directions as folks woke up and cleaned up their property from the storm. Trees and limbs would be scattered, along with pine needles and small branches.

He wanted to drill close enough to shore so that if he went through, he'd be able to make it out quick before the water got to him. But it was a good eight inches of ice there so he figured he'd be safe out deeper. He walked to the northern edge, where he knew the water was deepest. Up above was the cliff kids would jump from on hot summer days. The bottom was bottomless was what they said. If you kept sinking you would keep on sinking and never end up anywhere. He'd jumped that cliff many a time.

He wondered if Geneva ever had. He looked up at the cliff and saw her there, pushing her hair back behind her ears, raising both arms above her head so her ribs stuck out in relief below her breasts, and then she took a step forward and jumped down, down, and down. His eyes followed her descent and the spot where she entered into the water was where he would drill his hole. It would be as though he was making an opening for her escape. He was giving her breath and life and the thought that he was saving her once again made his work go quickly.

Plunker hoped the hole would be to her liking. He'd spent a good deal of time making sure it was the right width and that the edges were sculpted clean. It was a good hole. A hole to be proud of.

There were no fish in the quarry. But people dumped stuff there all the time—old cars, refrigerators—trash the dump wouldn't take without charging an arm and a leg. It also kept a secret, the quarry, if you needed it to.

Plunker sat back from his work and lit a cigarette. He looked up at the sun. It was getting late. He would make his way back to Geneva and let her know that the quarry was ready now.

THE ROOM GREW WARM as the day wore on, the air thick with sweat and sour breath and desperation. Geneva's thoughts stuck on one thing, only to slide onto the next just as quickly. It didn't help that Rick was a talker, his rant waffling back and forth between threatening and desperate. "I need to meet my connection in Montreal. He's expecting me," Rick said to Geneva.

"What're you connecting for?"

"He's got some merchandise for me," Rick said. He was lying. The connection was about the baby. Renee had told the truth. "By the looks of things, you could use a little cash infusion. Let me help you out."

"We're doing okay," Geneva said. "What kind of merchandise?"

Rick closed his eyes. Did not respond.

"Think of Marie," Renee pleaded. "Think what she would do." Geneva noted that Rick no longer looked in Renee's direction. She toyed with the idea of letting the two of them fight it out. Sticking them in a ring and seeing who would come out the victor. This was not practical, however. People tended to ask questions about a body.

"I'm not leaving here without that baby," Rick said. "So we're clear."

"I hear you," Geneva said and handed Cheri the gun to take over the watch. "You're not exactly in a bargaining position, though." Geneva left the room then so she could better think things through.

She went out to the store and took to pacing. The money would help set the store back in order and she could use it to pay off Renee so that things would be as they should be: Her and Cheri owning the store, running it together. No more pressure or stress or worry. Renee could be out of their lives for good.

This baby meant nothing to her. Who had looked after her when she was that small? No one, that's who. Wasn't until Auntie Marie took her in that things started getting better.

But Auntie Marie had stepped in and had protected her. And Auntie Marie would have protected the baby, would have taken her in as though her own.

It was clear that Geneva had to go forward with her plan. There was only one answer, like all of the lessons in her life were leading to this moment.

THE SKY OPENED UP brightly with the rays of God's love shining down. Iris would go out into the world and cleanse herself in this whiteness. She opened the door to the cabin and felt not the cold of the air, but the clarity of the light on her skin. It was needles and knives, sloughing away all that was old and dirty. She would become a child again herself. She would lead them all to salvation.

She was to follow the road, to go in search of her lost children. It was not until she had collected them all that she would be redeemed.

11

GENEVA LEFT THEM—took the man and the baby and was gone. Before she left she told Cheri to watch Renee. "Make sure she doesn't leave," Geneva said, handing Cheri the rifle. Then she took Renee's car keys for insurance.

Cheri was hungover and confused. There was all of this talk of the baby and what to do with the baby and Cheri could not focus on what was happening. She didn't know what Geneva was going to do and Renee kept asking her. Each time she replied, "Hell if I know." Images from the night before kept flashing in her brain—skin, teeth, hair—but then they would fly away just as quick.

They moved from the bedroom to the main living area where Renee paced, clasping and unclasping her hands. "We need a tree," she said. "And some Christmas carols."

"Knock yourself out," Cheri said. She opened the fridge in hopes of finding some beer but it was nearly empty, so she went to the store to grab a six pack. Geneva had locked up and put up the closed sign before she left. The store was quiet. She took a six pack out of the cooler and brought it over to the counter, twisted off a cap and drank several gulps before letting out a belch. "Much better," she said out loud.

She drank more and listened to her mother in the other room, softly singing Christmas carols. Silent night, holy night. But all was not calm. The door rattled in the wind.

IT WAS DONE. Cree was lost to her. Renee felt the grief settle into her chest—oddly, it felt the same as the baby did, nuzzled against her. There would never be another baby. Not one born to her and not one come to her so easily. The grief, she knew, would stay with her for the rest of her life. There was nothing she could do. She was trapped. Geneva had taken her keys. The phone had been removed.

She could leave and walk up the road to another house, but what then? Renee had failed again. This baby was lost. "You are lost," she said, looking into a reflection in the window and hoping to see the baby's trusting face, but seeing her own face looking back instead.

RICK DROVE AS GENEVA GAVE DIRECTIONS, the baby tucked into Geneva's arms. In their haste, they had forgotten the car seat. Rick almost suggested they go back for it, but decided it didn't matter in the long run. It would be bulky for him to carry through the snow. The less baggage the better.

She told him that her friend Plunker knew the path best and so he followed behind them on his ATV. They would lead him, Geneva said, until they got to a point where he would have to go forward on his own. "We can't go where you're going," she said. "You have to go alone." He had five thousand dollars in the duffle bag in his trunk—had gotten it from his mother's bank account before leaving town. He was going to give Geneva half of it for her troubles, he said. He also promised her he'd be back with some cash for her once the deal was done. Of course, that would never happen. He never planned on seeing this crazy, one-armed bitch again. As soon as he got to Montreal and got rid of the baby, his plan was to be on the next plane out—but not back to Florida. Maybe California or Mexico. He'd been smart about bringing a passport. His money would stretch farther there and when it ran out, he could find work at a resort. People would love him in Mexico. Thoughts of the sunny warmth pushed away the cloying cold.

She said that she had arranged for a car to meet him on the other side of the trail in a few hours time. "The guy who's meeting you is a good guy," she said. "He'll wait all day for you if he has to."

When he questioned her about why he couldn't go through the border like regular folks. "I've got the birth certificate," he reminded her. "The baby's mine to do with what I please."

"But you've also got a record, right? I mean, I'm just speculating here. But you seem like the sort."

"Sure," he said. "Yeah."

"Border patrol isn't too friendly to ex-cons crossing here," she said, "especially not with a baby in a carseat and a bag of cash in the trunk."

She made good sense. No dummy this one. He would give her the benefit of the doubt. "Sounds like a plan then," Rick said, but he would have said anything. She was freeing him and soon he'd have his money and once he had that everything would be easier. Money made life simple, he believed, though he'd never had enough of it to know for sure.

They were going to leave his car behind for him, too, so that he could find his way back out after the deal was done. She promised him she'd come and check on it, turn the engine over. He hadn't thought to ask her about why he couldn't leave the car parked in her lot. Not until they were almost there—but the question died in his mouth.

"There it is," she said, and directed him to a barely visible cut off in the trees. The snow was high but not impassable. There were tire tracks from a smaller vehicle which had already blazed the way. "Drive back as far as you can," she said. "Don't worry about getting stuck. Plunker can get you out." Rick looked in his rear view mirror to see the fellow on the ATV close behind them.

His dash clock said it was going on 3:00 p.m. Dark would be coming soon and he would be alone in these woods with the baby. He would be on his way to freedom.

PLUNKER LED THE WAY, Rick in the middle, and Geneva picking up the rear with the baby in a sling she had fashioned from an old blanket. She offered to carry the child this first round so that Rick might conserve his energy. Rick seemed grateful for this suggestion.

The woods were quiet, the wind having settled down, the animals digging in for the cold night ahead. Before they left, Geneva gave Plunker a backpack to carry. "It's going to be heavy," she warned him, "but it's only going to be heavy on the way in." The pack weighed him down and so the going was slower than they expected. She wanted to yell ahead, tell him to hurry, but held her tongue.

What she needed was patience.

There was yet enough light so she could make out all the lines of the trees and the whiteness of the snow against the blue silhouettes in front of her. They made it to the opening which led to the quarry before the sun set. A mile had never taken so long before.

"Terry," she called ahead. "Let's rest." Plunker turned and nodded. Made his way back to where they were standing.

"It's pretty here," Rick said, turning and smiling at Geneva. For a second she was almost won over by him. He was so like a young boy noticing the beauty of this place. "But too damn cold. Let's keep moving, yeah?"

"No," she said. "We're almost there."

Plunker removed the backpack and dropped it at his feet. He stood next to Geneva. "Damn, woman," he said. "What you got in that thing anyway? Rocks?" She did not join his banter. Instead she bent down and opened the pack, pulled out some rope.

"Get his hands," she said to Plunker. "Behind his back." Plunker took the rope from her and held it loosely in his hands. Rick's mouth opened to speak but nothing came out. Above them a hawk circled and called, dove out of sight behind a patch of tall white pines.

"What's going on?" Rick said.

"Go tie him," Geneva said. "Do it."

When Plunker grabbed Rick, they struggled. Geneva pulled the handgun out of her pocket. Lifted her arm up and shot it into the sky. The baby startled and whimpered. The men stopped dead and Plunker gained the upper hand.

IRIS'S FEET FELT ON FIRE as though she were walking across coals and not down the icy road. It had taken her longer than she anticipated to get half a mile from home. Her children would be close by, she could feel them. They were not answering her plaintive calls, but she knew they would soon give up this silly game of hide and seek.

In the distance she saw them moving toward her disguised as white and yellow lights, tunneling through the air. Iris moved out onto the road and opened her arms to welcome them into the most loving of mother hugs. They had returned to her. They were all finally home.

AS THE ROPES TIGHTENED around Rick's wrists, he realized that her intention was that he not make it out of these woods alive. Oddly, he thought of the baby—used her as an impetus for forward motion. He felt a tingling realization that he was responsible for her—for bringing her onto this earth. Maybe the choice he had made had been wrong. Maybe Renee would take him back. They could patch things up and move on, raise the child as their own.

"What about the baby?" he called. "What about my child? You going to leave her fatherless?"

"You're the one who's doing that, Mister," Geneva said. "Not me."

He had been right to fear the woods all these years. To dream of the darkness and of wolves chasing him. To know that someday he would die alone in dark woods.

He gasped at the cold air. He needed to do something, to fight for his life. He was conscious that he had never wanted to live more than he wanted to live in these moments when he realized he was about to die. His heart throbbed with fear. He would not die. He would fight for his life.

"Help," Rick called. "Somebody help." Geneva pulled a bandana out of the bag and handed it to Plunker.

"Here," she said. "For his mouth." Rick screamed again but she knew no one would hear him. Folks were far away and even if his voice carried they were in their barns milking, or inside their warm kitchens cooking dinner, baking meat pies, preparing for Christmas Eve Mass. No one would pay him any mind.

Plunker gagged Rick and the screams were reduced to muted grunts, whimpers. Her heart felt them but she would not let her mind feel them. She thought of herself as a baby instead, alone and scared. Her mother might have sold her off, too, if she'd ever thought of it.

"Let's bring him closer to the edge," she said to Plunker. "Will be easier to get him onto the ice after."

"After what?" Plunker said, turning to her, losing his hold on the bound man.

Rick, arms tied behind him, took off running, slipping, the snow cushioning his fall, getting back up and running again.

"Shit," Geneva said. "You're going to have to help me. Get over here."

Plunker ran to her side. She took aim with the gun. "Get behind me," she said. "Get close and put your arms around me. Use one to hold the baby's head tight against my chest." Plunker did as he was told. "Use your other hand to steady my arm," she said. Rick was running but kept losing his balance on the slippery ground. He was not so far away that she didn't have a good shot.

IRIS'S CHILDREN MET HER in an explosion of bright lights, ice, and snow. The pain at first was like that excruciating moment of labor, as the crowning head is pushing through, making its way toward the light, and then her body moved into the moment of pure, exquisite joy that is relief and the end of all pain. Forever.

RICK WAS FREE. He had made it. All he had to do was get far enough away from them and back to the road and he would be safe. He had seen houses in the distance and he knew the people would help him. They would have to.

He was safe. He would live. He made a vow that he would not sell the baby. If God let him live, he would do everything in his power to make a nice life for the child. He would not be bad anymore. He would be good. He would be.

———

PLUNKER STOOD AS DIRECTED and breathed in the scent of her hair—tangy wood smoke. He wished the circumstances were different and that he was hugging her for real, but this was good enough. "Okay," she said. "Keep steady."

Plunker heard the explosion, felt the recoil, and watched as the man went down. Geneva left his embrace and took off on a jog with the handgun, caught up to the downed man, and shot him twice in the head. A fine red spray covered the snow. The baby wailed in fright at the noise, her cries covering the echoing gunshots.

THE FIRST BULLET did not hurt him so much as it stunned him. She had really done it. Really shot him. Rick almost laughed at the absurdity of it. He should have been in Florida, behind the bar at Titty's mocking his Christmas bonus.

There was an instant after that second bullet that he still held onto hope—he could make it. It was Christmas Eve. Surely she would not kill him on Christmas Eve.

And then there was another bullet and nothing.

IT WASN'T UNTIL the noise stopped that Plunker realized they had killed a man. They. He had been a part of it. Held her arm steady while she aimed. As good as pulled the trigger himself. He looked at his hands, red and raw and shaking, thought of his woman back home by the fire and wished he'd not left her that morning. Geneva turned to him and motioned him over. "Bring the pack," Geneva said. "Hurry."

Moving on instinct now, Plunker picked up the pack and

brought it to her. Inside she had some bricks and more rope. "We need to weigh him down," she said.

He helped her and though one part of him realized that doing so was making things worse, he knew he had to help. Otherwise he was going to jail.

Jail. Prison. That's where his mother told him he'd end up one day if he wasn't careful. "Don't turn out like your daddy," his mother had warned, poking her index finger at his forehead. "Use that mind of yours to think."

Geneva set the crying baby down on the blanket nearby. Then she went to work and wrapped a piece of old tarp around the man's wounds to stop them from leaking so much blood and then they tied him up tightly against the bricks and dragged him over the ice. "Good hole," she said when they found it. "Perfect hole." Earlier he would have been thrilled to hear these words but now he wished she would take them back.

Before they slid the man over the edge, Geneva dug in his pocked and pulled out the wallet and car keys. She took the cash out of the wallet and held it out to Plunker. "Here," she said. It was several hundred dollars. "Take it."

Plunker shook his head no. "Take it," she said. "I owe you." She did owe him, yes, but not this. "Take it." She shoved the money into his hand and he looked at it, then put it in his pocket. At least he would be able to get good and drunk. He would need to.

"Okay," she said. "Let's go." They bent over the body, slid it over the edge of the hole, and watched as it sunk out of sight. "We need to finish up and get out of here," Geneva said, straightening, wiping her palm on her pant leg. He would have liked a moment to say something—a prayer. Something. Some words for this dead man.

———

THE MAN WAS DEAD and there was nothing she could do to change it now. Geneva had killed him. It was time to get rid of the evidence. First they needed to cover the blood with snow, but really she wasn't too worried about it. Some animal would get to it and if not, it was hunting season and the spray and beaten down snow would appear as though someone had scored a buck. She searched the ground near where the body had been to make sure the other bullets hadn't traveled through.

They covered their tracks as best they could, backtracking to the car. Once at the car, she opened the trunk and took out the duffel bag of money and from the glove box, the baby's birth certificate. She left the keys on the seat, hoping someone would end up taking the car far away. Either way, cars were abandoned here all the time when folks skipped over the border. It would not be out of the ordinary, she didn't think, for this one to be found here. She wiped down the handgun and left it in the glove box and then wiped the car clean of other prints, though she had known to wear gloves to begin with.

All signs of the man were now erased. He was dead. And it was time for Mass.

12

IT WAS HARD TO HOLD onto Plunker with her one arm, duffle bag full of money and squirming baby wedged between the two of them. The road was hard and bumpy, faces thrust into the cold air, but she felt nothing. The only thing she was aware of was the sound of air exhaling from the man as he died, after the last of her shots rang away. Air leaving his body.

She had killed before, but animals only. She would often go hunting with Clint because she was a better shot than he was and they needed the meat. She did not like to do it, but it was necessary. Before this day, she had never even aimed a gun at another human being. Never even thought to. Not even Clint in the worst of times. She had not thought she was capable of such an act, such a sin.

This time, however, she wasn't sure of the necessity. It had seemed the only choice, the right choice, but now that it was done and the man gone from this world…

He was not meat; he was flesh. Body and blood.

A man had died that night, that Christmas Eve, by her hand. Someone would have to pay for it.

———

PLUNKER LEFT GENEVA behind in the parking lot. When she got off his ATV, he didn't give her a chance to get a sentence out. Instead he turned the handlebars and circled back onto the road home, gone. He never wanted to see her face or hear her voice again. She had bewitched him and things had not turned out the way they ought to have, the way he thought they would.

The evening sky was clear but with the smell of ice in the air. He imagined snow falling gently through the night, covering their tracks in the woods, covering the patches of blood, obliterating the evidence. He thought of the man sinking to the bottom of the hole, sinking gently until he reached the black pit that was the bottom of the quarry. Plunker squeezed his eyes tight closed and then opened them again, wishing he was waking from a dream, a nightmare, but instead he was in reality. There was the sky and there were the trees and there was the road and there his tires were moving along it.

He never should have left his woman that morning. Should have stayed with her and stoked the fire and made sure she was good and warm. He should not have left the cabin and because he had, he was being punished. As it should be. He had been swayed by the good looks of a woman, something his mother had always warned him against. "Women ain't good for nothing but a lay," she told him. "You only need to keep one good one and leave the rest alone."

For most of his life he'd heeded that advice—until now. He would pay the price. He knew he would. A few more miles and he would be home. He had no Christmas gift for his woman, but he hoped that having him home beside her would be gift enough.

———

"WHERE'RE YOU GOING?" Cheri asked when she saw Renee in one of Marie's old parkas.

Renee loved Christmas carols, she remembered, which is partly why Cheri hated them. In a classic example of the duality of her mother's psyche, the woman used to listen to Christmas music all year long—said it was her favorite music—though she often seemed ambivalent about the actual celebration of the birth of the Christ child. As a child, Cheri had wanted to clap her hands over her ears to drown out the songs.

Once, her mother set up the tree on Christmas morning and Cheri had to help with the decorations and with wrapping her own gifts. "Santa doesn't exist," her mother had said to her. "You know that right?" Well, she had and she hadn't known it, but her mother should have kept quiet about it regardless. Who told a five-year-old there was no Santa? Who did that?

In fact, she hated Christmas in general. The ho-ho-ho of it. The sing-songy falseness. The peace and the joy and the love. The baby Jesus, the wise men, Frosty, Rudolph, the frankincense, the tinsel—all of it—every last single spingly-spangly bit of it—could go straight to hell.

"If I have to sit here for one more second waiting, I'm going to use that gun on myself," Renee said. "I'm going to the woods to get us a tree."

Cheri shrugged. "Suit yourself."

RENEE HEADED OUT BACK of the store to the woods there, down to a stand that her father had grown especially for Christmas trees. She walked in among the trees and looked for the right one. "Here it is," she said to herself. "I found it."

It didn't take much work for her to chop a notch out with the axe and then saw through the tree as her father had taught her to do all those years ago. Briefly, she allowed herself to picture future Christmases with Cree—next year there would be lots of presents and good food, music and parties and colored lights. Cree would grow up knowing she was loved and wanted and all of this would culminate on Christmas mornings stretching far into the future.

But then, no. Cree was gone. Did her no good to fantasize.

The tree came down softly on the hard-packed snow. She took up its base and pulled it behind her back to the house. Already, the fragrant odor of sap, the blood of the tree, lifted her mood. She would make the best of whatever was ahead of her. She had no choice but to do so.

THERE WAS THE SHERIFF'S CAR and an ambulance both with their lights off and a cluster of men out milling around in Plunker's yard when he got home. He would have driven right on by to avoid the lot of them if the sheriff hadn't noticed him and waved him over.

His heart clenched up tight. She'd done it. Turned him in. Sure he could say that she was responsible but no one would believe it. He had only held her arm steady as she shot, but he was the one who drilled the hole. He was the one who had done that. The hole proved everything. That he was involved. That he was an accomplice to murder. Plunker was done for and what he worried about most in those moments was who would take care of his woman. Who would keep her warm?

He parked his ATV and sat on it, waiting. He would not go to them, would not make it easy on them. They would have to drag him off his vehicle, would have to cuff him against his will, kicking and screaming and biting if he had to. The sheriff walked over alone, leaving the other men behind, smoking their cigarettes.

"Got some bad news for you," the sheriff said, putting a hand on Plunker's back.

"What'd I do now?" Plunker chuckled and held his hands out in front of him, awaiting the inevitable handcuffs the man would place on them. No sense after all in fighting it.

"As best we can tell she'd been drinking," the sheriff said, "and wandered out of the house…" Plunker jumped off the ATV and ran to the cabin, threw open the door and called out for his woman. *Iris? Iris?* The walls echoed his calls. He looked in each of the small rooms and found them empty. He ran back to the door and stood facing the sheriff, panting white hot breaths into the frigid air.

The sheriff helped him to sit on the steps and kept a firm hand on his shoulder. "She's dead, son," he said. "The plow was out scraping the pavement clean and she was standing there right out in the middle of the road, buck naked. Hit her. Knocked her clear up into the snow bank." Plunker's body shuddered. "It was an accident," the man said. "You know those plows, hard to see out of and they can't stop for nothing. Damn brakes are shot."

Plunker was done and he was done. In less than twenty-four hours he had killed two whole people. People who had once lived and now were dead. He thought of his woman earlier that day, how peaceful her face had seemed while she sat by the fire. He thought she might have looked like the Virgin Mary, waiting for something grand, something miraculous to happen.

GENEVA FOUND CHERI sitting by the stove drinking a beer. Geneva walked to the couch and dropped the duffle bag at her feet. "Where's

Renee?"

"Out chopping down a Christmas tree," Cheri said.

"I've got to put this baby down," Geneva said. She left Cheri and found the small bed that Renee had left made up for the baby. Geneva placed Cree gently on her back and left her and then headed for her own bedroom where she lay down on top of the covers.

On her bedside table were her compact disc player and headphones. She hit play and put the headphones on, listened to Christmas music—Nat King Cole, Bing Crosby. She pictured the store shelves as she sometimes did when she tried to sleep at night—went through each item and tried to tally a mental inventory. Now, the items were unclear, she had not been keeping track. Had no idea, for instance, whether they needed to order more flour. Everything was falling apart. In her mind, the shelves crumbled, the items upon them crashing down, littering the once clean floor, now covered in the blood that she had spilled.

His woman was in the ambulance covered over with a sheet. They had tried to revive her, they told him, but it didn't work. "You're lucky you caught us," the sheriff told him. They had been about to leave for the morgue when they heard the whine of his ATV in the distance. They were doing him a favor by waiting around so he could say goodbye. A favor.

Plunker looked up and noted that no smoke was coming out of the chimney. She'd let the fire die down. He wondered if he would need to bring in more wood. His mind flashed on the mist of red hovering over the man's body before it covered the snow surrounding him.

"Can I see her?" Plunker asked.

"Well," the sheriff said, shaking his head. "It's not pretty."

"Didn't expect it would be," Plunker said. The man nodded and led him over to the ambulance. One of the EMTs opened the door for him and told him to watch himself on the stairs.

Inside the ambulance was gloomy. He saw the shape of his woman beneath a blue sheet. He put one hand on her forehead. It wasn't enough. He pulled back the sheet and exposed her face, darkened by bruises, battered, but otherwise he thought she looked pretty good, calm even. He regretted that he had never seen her look so when she was alive. The skin of her cheek was hardening with cold and rigor. He touched once and then pulled his fingers back. He hoped she would think of him with fondness. Hoped she would not blame him for her death. He bent and kissed her lips, wanting to find them soft and giving but finding them hard instead, he recoiled and touched his fingers to his own mouth. Plunker covered her face and left the ambulance.

When he climbed down off the ambulance steps, the sheriff came over to him.

"I'm sorry, son," the sheriff said, and gave Plunker one soft thump on the back. "You go get yourself a beer now."

When the vehicles drove away, he stood for a long time in his driveway, listening to the wind tickling the bare branches above, waiting for something, but he was not sure what. He stuck his hands in his pockets and touched the money he'd jammed in there earlier. He could go out in search of booze but found instead that he could not make himself.

They might have a bottle or two of blackberry brandy hidden in kitchen somewhere. Inside, the cabin was still, the way it was when he came home late on a summer afternoon, his woman out back napping off the day's heat. He went to the kitchen area and rummaged around in the cabinets until he found a half pint with a few swallows still in it.

Plunker moved to the chairs in the main room and sat down. He ran his hands over the rough fabric covering the arms of the chair he sat in. It was an easy chair which swiveled and rocked and had belonged to his mother. The thing had gotten so much use over the years that the arm upholstery had worn clear off. His woman had sewn on these rough patches, woolly and harsh, and they had kept the thing intact.

The stove was cold to the touch. Plunker felt weary then. Too weary to start a fire. Too weary to consider when it was he last slept or ate.

He opened the bottle and took a swallow. Let his head rest back against the seat. He could have slept. Easy he could have. His eyelids lowered and he reached his hand out to place the bottle on the small table next to his chair. His hand brushed up against something and his eyes opened. It was a present. A Christmas gift from his woman to him. There was a small card on the wrapping paper written in her jagged block letters, "For Plunker, my lover."

He lifted the package close to his face and read the words again and again until his eyes went soft. He slid his finger under the tape and opened up the wrapping. She had knit him a thick pair of wool socks. They would keep his feet warm for the rest of the winter. She had thought to do this for him and he'd done nothing for her except leave her alone and let her die.

Plunker had done many bad things in his life but nothing had ever made him feel worse than losing his woman. He lifted the socks up to his nose and breathed in.

He should start a fire. It was dark and getting colder out. He thought of Geneva, how unmoved she seemed by the day's events. She had not even shed a tear. That one was built from other stuff than most people—hard stuff, iron ore. It was as though she hadn't heard the sound the man made when he fell to the ground, hadn't heard his last muffled breath.

The sheriff would be back for him sometime soon. He knew it was only a matter of time before Geneva fessed up. He was done. And he should be done. He'd killed two people on that day.

He took the last sip of brandy, let it warm his core, the warmth tingling out to his limbs. Nothing was right now. And there was nothing he could do to make things so.

Plunker clutched the socks his woman had given him in his fist and let his head roll back and closed his eyes. Sleep. But sleep would not find him. Instead he heard his mother in his head, telling him to make things right. Telling him something about redemption.

His mother had not been perfect but she had tried to be good. Tried to do the right thing. She would want him to make things as right as he could. She would tell him that faith in God would make things right again. Only He could sit in judgment and offer Plunker freedom from this wrongdoing. Plunker stood and left the cabin, got back on his ATV and drove into the darkness. He would seek his answers among the stars.

The woods were still. He was as much a part of the woods as the trees were. Plunker was at the man's car quickly. His hands felt too cold to grip anything, the warmth from the brandy long since gone from his body. It was a false warmth anyway—one that could kill you with the cold if you believed in it. He inserted the key and turned the ignition on and waited for the heat.

From his pocket he pulled out the wrapping paper from his gift. He dug around in the glove box and found the gun and a stub of a pencil. He took time writing the note, explaining how he had come upon this man and killed him in hopes of getting his money. "I done this horrible act by myself," Plunker wrote, "I offer my own life in exchange for this man's. And that is all I have to give." He wrote about how he had drilled the hole, how he had tricked the fellow into the woods. How he had planned it all. With each word he wrote, Plunker felt himself swell up with thoughts of his woman and the dead man and how with each word he wrote they were forgiving him.

When he was finished writing, he read the note again and placed it beside him on the passenger seat. He warmed his stiff fingers by the heater until they were limber and when they were, he cracked his knuckles, picked up the handgun, put the muzzle in his mouth, and pulled the trigger.

In that flash of a second, he felt his body jump off the cliff, falling, falling into the water below, deep into the quarry, deep into the black where all was lost and all was forgiven.

13

IT HAD BEEN NIGHT, late while people were sleeping, when Geneva had come to live with Auntie Marie. She had been the one who called the police for help. 911 like she learned from television. Dial 911. And when they ask what is your emergency, you tell them exactly what it is and where you are.

Her emergency had been that her mother was sick.

Was she breathing? Yes.

Was she awake? Yes.

Was she able to speak? Yes.

Did she seem hot to the touch? No.

Had she been vomiting? No.

When pushed, Geneva admitted there were no physical manifestations of the illness. Rather, it was that her mother could no longer see Geneva. She seemed not to care whether her daughter lived or breathed or ate or washed her hair.

She was gone.

Finally, the dispatcher understood and along with the ambulance came a social worker, who took Geneva away. Her mother had not even said goodbye. Instead, she lay placidly and let them strap her onto a gurney and wheel her out of the trailer. It was over like that.

CHERI SAT WHERE RENEE HAD LEFT HER, except now she was entertaining the baby on her lap, paging through *People* magazine and pointing out which stars had gained and which lost weight.

"She's back?" Renee said, moving to them, touching Cree's cheek and then Cheri's, who flinched away from the touch.

"Yeah," Cheri said.

"What about the others?" Renee asked.

Cheri shrugged, tightened her grip on the baby. "Geneva went to bed. I guess that guy is gone or something."

"Gone? Where?"

"How am I supposed to know?" Cheri said, slapping shut the magazine. "Away."

The grief which had attached itself to Renee lifted and flew off into the distance, above the trees and the hills, far up north where it would stay. She was free. "I'm going to get the decorations," she said. She could remember where they were in the basement, three boxes carefully labeled—colored balls, lights, a crèche.

GENEVA WOKE TO THE SOUND of Renee's voice, giddy in the front room. The crack of boxes opening and closing, soda bottles fizzing. She could smell the wood crackling in the fire and also a new scent, fresh cut pine. She sat bolt upright and readied herself to go out there and be a part of whatever was going on. What she remembered was that it was Christmas Eve.

Then she remembered it was one unlike any other. Her arm was gone. Clint was gone. Auntie Marie was gone. And someone else was gone. Another person, who had once woken up as a child on Christmas morning with all of the anticipation and glow, was also dead.

Her stomach clenched tight and she lay back down, pulled the covers up. She felt as alone as she had felt when her mother left in the ambulance. Standing, as she had been, in the dirt driveway with the social worker's hand hot on her back. "Let's get going," the woman had said. "We'll pack up a few of your things and then be off."

There hadn't been much to pack. A few pieces of clothing. Some photographs. She knew enough to pack light, that she would be back.

And then they had driven out of the boundaries of her town into another. The lights had been on in the store when they pulled up. Auntie Marie was expecting them.

"This lady's been waiting a long time for the right kid to come stay with her," the social worker said. "I think that kid is you, don't you?"

"I guess," Geneva said. She was unsure why anyone would wait for her, would want her.

The social worker shut off the engine, opened her car door and got out. Geneva followed because there was nothing else to do.

The woman who met them was quiet. She was calm. She reminded Geneva of an image she had seen once of three children and a woman hanging in the sky. She was a woman who came to them in a vision. She spoke to the children and told them not to be afraid. She told them she came from heaven. She told them they, too, would go to heaven if they prayed and made sacrifices. She was the lady of the rosary. She was Fatima.

"I'm Marie," the woman said, holding out her hand to Geneva. "You're safe here." She was wearing a long, pink housecoat, so old and threadbare that it seemed to glow whitely in the light.

The social worker left them soon after they arrived. And Geneva stood by while Marie made up a bed for her on the couch. "You'll sleep here tonight," she said. "Tomorrow we'll get you set up in your own room." After the woman got her settled in her bed, she left Geneva alone, but all she wanted was for the woman to come back again and touch her gently on the forehead as she had done before. A touch that had both burned and soothed.

CHERI DID NOT PARTAKE of the tree decoration. Instead, she sat with the baby on her lap and watched as her mother hung the old ornaments—mostly glass balls, but some that she and Geneva had made when they were children. Even some that her mother and Auntie Marie had made.

The tree was a slice of their family history—as messed up as it was. All of them mashed together, represented by childish hands: a flat stone painted red and green with a piece of yellow yarn attached to it, a snowflake cut out of paper and glued onto cardboard. Macaroni sprayed silver and gold applied to many different objects. This was their tree, their life.

The baby grabbed Cheri's index finger and stuck it in her mouth, gummed it. "She's hungry," Renee said, turning from the tree with a clumped handful of tinsel. "You might fix her a bottle."

"I don't know how," Cheri said, pulling her finger out of the baby's mouth and wiping it on her pant leg.

"I'll fix it then," Renee said. "And you can feed her." Cheri thought to protest but decided against it. What would be the harm of giving one bottle?

"Here," Renee said, handing Cheri the bottle. Cheri weighed the bottle in her hand and let Renee maneuver the baby into the proper position for her. "Tilt it," Renee said, angling Cheri's wrist. The baby puckered her mouth and accepted the nipple. With one hand she held onto the bottle and with her other hand reached up and grasped Cheri's wrist. She was touched by the simplicity of this—that it asked nothing of her other than these moments of closeness.

FROM HER BED GENEVA HEARD the knocking on the door, the extra set of feet entering the house. She got up and went to the door of her room, cracked it open. Down the hall she saw Renee and Cheri standing together with the sheriff.

He asked them about the man. Said his car had been spotted at the store earlier.

"He's my ex," Renee said. "We're still friendly, though. He was planning on spending Christmas with us, but then he took off and hasn't showed back up yet. Figure he's out somewhere tying on a good one." Renee was a good liar, but Geneva went lightheaded regardless. Her bare feet ached on the cold painted floor, grit and small stones digging into the tender skin, but she would not move.

"I'm sorry to tell you but we think your fella's passed on," the sheriff said, placing a calming hand on Renee's shoulder. The hand then went down her arm, clasped her hand, squeezed. The sheriff was making his claim for the future. Letting Renee know he was able if she was willing.

"Dead?" Renee said, her face blanched, contorted. She was very good. She had to have known what Geneva had planned for him and why he had not returned with her. She had to have. Cheri and Renee glanced at each other with the news. Stupid. If the sheriff had seen that look between them they'd all be done for.

"Much as we can tell," the sheriff said. "Bucky Tilton was out ski-dooing and found a car with out of state plates in the woods by the quarry." The sheriff stretched a knot out of his back. He turned to Cheri. Cheri smiled to cover the panic that was creeping up her body. "Terry Plunker was inside." Cheri opened her mouth to speak but nothing came out. "Took his own life right in the other fella's car," the sheriff said. "Said he was the one who killed this other fella, but we don't know if that's true or not. He was awful upset the last time I seen him. Investigation's still open." And then she knew without a doubt what Geneva had done. "The other fella's in the quarry. Divers went in but can't see a damn thing in that murky water. Then they hung some fancy cameras down there and got a good look at him." The sheriff handed Rene a photo. Rick's face ghostly and green and terrified. Dead, no doubt dead. "I know it's not the best photo, but does that look about right?" Renee nodded and coughed. "Good. Need to notify the next of kin. Was hoping one of you might have that information."

"There's his mother," Renee said. "And me."

"Got a number for that mother?" The sheriff took a notepad and pencil out of his jacket pocket, licked the tip of the pencil, prepared to write.

"Now listen," Renee said, placing a hand on the sheriff's arm, "she's not right in the head. I better call her myself. That way I can break it to her easy."

The sheriff nodded, put his pad and pencil away, clearly relieved to not have to phone this stranger.

RICK WAS DEAD. Tears pinched at the corners of Renee's eyes. She looked to Cheri who had Cree slung on her hip, looking natural with the child, a young mother. She looked back in the direction of the sheriff who was still talking, giving them probably more details about a crime scene than he should have. But then the case might have been all cut and dried to him. A man had come to their village and the town misfit had killed him for his cash and then killed himself. End of story.

She turned her head slightly and looked down the hall. There she saw Geneva's door ajar and in the darkness, the one-armed figure hunched there, small and powerless. Their eyes met and Geneva eased the door shut. Renee heard the click of the latch.

When she was pregnant with Cheri, Renee had felt the world was clothed in wool, muted from her. Breathing did not come easily, lungs compressed, pushed in, and mucus membranes swollen, making the clear passage of air unsuccessful. Actions once simple— walking up stairs, folding laundry, loading stock onto the shelves— were labored and light-headed movements done only with a great deal of forethought. She had not enjoyed the experience of being with child as she thought women were supposed to. And Marie had no knowledge to help her, never having given birth herself.

She had had to look through the encyclopedias in the library at school to learn about how the egg is fertilized in her fallopian tubes before it falls into the uterus and latches on. From the book, she learned about her child's development, month by month, amazed at this creature living inside her. And then when she felt the movements, at first tantalizing and joyous and then frightening and life-altering, she had understood that she would truly be a mother to another living being. It was then that she thought about turning off what emotion might have existed. She should not let herself become attached to the child. She would fail at motherhood. Eventually, she would need to leave.

She wondered if it had been because she was so young herself, a child, really, and fearful of the world finding out her shame. But even when people did find out, not much came of it. People had already treated her a certain way, so that didn't change.

Who is the father? Marie wanted to know over and over again

and would not be satisfied when Renee told her she didn't know. It might have been her driver's ed teacher or the Canadian man who had screwed her in the store's bathroom on his way home from the lake, his children waiting patiently in their station wagon outside. It might have been the man whose A-frame she had gone to. It could have been anyone. Cheri had never asked, intuiting there was no answer she wanted to hear.

Who is the father?

Cree might one day ask her this question. And what would Renee say about the father—that he had gone away or even that he had died. He was gone.

AFTER THE SHERIFF LEFT, Cheri went to Geneva's door, leaving her mother to wrap herself in grief and horror.

She didn't knock. She opened the door and entered, shutting it behind her. She went to Geneva's bed and sat on it. "What have you done?" she said. Geneva remained still, her back to Cheri.

"I did what I had to do," Geneva said.

"And you got Plunker involved." Cheri's face grew hot. "And now he's dead." She let go unsaid the last words. The words that clung in her mouth—for you. Everything for you.

"I can't stop a man from doing what he chooses to do. I wouldn't even begin to know how to try."

"You used him to do your dirty work," Cheri said. "He was just a man. A human being."

"He wanted to do it," Geneva said. "He practically begged me."

"I don't believe you," Cheri said, shaking her head. She couldn't imagine that murder had been the only answer and that Plunker had been so willing a participant. He'd always seemed like a decent guy when he came in the store. He was interested in her tattoos. "There must have been something else you could have done."

"Trust me. There was no other way," Geneva said, quiet but angry. "You always think there's some other way, but there isn't. There are lots of choices but only one way. At least that's true for people like me."

"What's that supposed to mean? People like you?"

"Forget it," Geneva said. "I'm tired now." She lay back down and pulled the covers tight around her.

"You killed someone." Cheri was close to hysteria. "You killed two people. That man and Plunker. It's your fault." Geneva moved quickly, came around Cheri from behind and clasped her hand over her mouth.

"Quiet," she whispered in Cheri's ear. "You know nothing. You saw nothing. You heard nothing. Don't say anything." Cheri struggled against Geneva's grip but she was strong, one arm or not. Finally she pulled away.

"I'm not going to lie for you," Cheri said.

Geneva stared hard at Cheri for what seemed a long time until she turned away. It was time for Cheri to go.

CHERI AND HER MOTHER SAT side by side on the couch, the baby sleeping between them. Midnight approached and passed by. Not until the grandfather clock struck did her mother turn to her and say, "Merry Christmas."

"Yeah," Cheri said. But nothing felt merry—not the blinking tree lights, not the carols.

ON HER FIRST MORNING with Marie, Geneva had stirred to the sound of adults—two women—drinking coffee, eating breakfast, utensils scraping against plates. Whispered talk of who would do what that day. Of how the other woman would watch the store so that Marie could take care of her, the girl as she was called. "She's a pretty one," Marie said. "Probably too much so for her own good."

Geneva swelled at being called pretty. No one had ever said something so gentle about her before. Her mother's boyfriends had eyed her and commented on her various parts—but their talk was rough and ugly. Their talk meant it was only a matter of time before one of them came hunting her.

She dozed again, thinking of her loveliness. Hoping it was true.

She awoke later to a girl kneeling by her head, staring into her face. "You have sleep in your eyes," the girl said. Geneva lifted her hand to wipe the gunk out of the corners of her eyes. "Your fingernails are gross. Come with me."

The girl helped her get up from the couch and pulled her into the bathroom. There she turned on the tap and rubbed the nail scrubber on a bar of Ivory soap on the counter. She took Geneva's hands one by one in her own and scrubbed beneath the nails until they were clean. It hurt but Geneva dared not say a word. "There," the girl said, holding up Geneva's hands for inspection. "Now you're clean. Much better, right?"

"Yes," Geneva said. The girl dropped Geneva's hands and held out her own.

"I'm Cheri," she said, and took Geneva's hand in her own and shook it. "I'm your new sister."

AUNTIE MARIE CAME TO GENEVA while she lay in her bed. Clothed in a blue dress covered in bright stars, she said, "St. Ignatius begged the good people of the Roman Catholic Church to show him no charity. He begged for his own martyrdom to be complete. He desired nothing more than to bleed for his God. You have shown me none of this desire."

"I did what I thought you would want me to do," Geneva said. "I saved the baby's life." She wanted to move from where she lay but found she could not, that her limbs were frozen in place.

"You shed your thin skin of belief too easily in the face of desire and disapproval. How can you ask me to condone that? I'll show you no charity." With these words and Auntie Marie was gone. Geneva got up and dressed herself, left the room and sneaked to the back door. She heard the others in the front room still—not talking so much as moving around, occupying the same space. She left the house and took to the woods.

When she got to the old fire pit, she lay prostrate on the icy ground. Cold night air made its way down the length of her body. She felt none of it.

"Come back," she said, her voice muffled by snow. She turned over and spread her arms and legs out at her sides. It was there. Her arm back and whole. She clenched both fists and released them. The stars above moved closer and covered her over, landing on her clothing and exposed skin until they burned into her palms and the soles of her feet. The stars cut through, forming the most perfect, the most beautiful wounds upon her.

Geneva rose from the ground long after the stars retreated and inspected her palms and feet. There, there, there, there. She saw the sign left behind. Geneva was adorned with the sign of the most holy. Upon her hands and feet were the bleeding wounds of the stigmata. Along with these wounds, the words came in fits of bright light and pinches in her belly, telling her what to do next.

She would leave some of Rick's money behind for Cheri and Renee. She would let them know what bills to pay if they so chose. Let them know what to take care of to keep things running. After all, the store belonged to them as much as it did to her. She no longer needed the shackles it had provided.

IT WAS THE FIRST TIME in years Cheri had been in a house with a Christmas tree. In the city, she never allowed herself such things. Instead she went out with whoever was around on Christmas Eve and got plastered, helped close the bars, was among the alone and the lonely. She still was not convinced that wasn't a better way to live. No ties. Nothing to stress over, no one's feelings to worry about.

Today she would try it out again and see how it felt on her—this being around people, around family. She would give Geneva this one last shot and if things didn't seem better to her by New Year's Eve, she'd be gone—whether her mother stayed around or not was irrelevant.

She put on pajama bottoms and a sweatshirt and left her room. In the kitchen, she found Renee with the baby on her lap, sitting stiffly in one of the kitchen chairs, eating breakfast with a place set for Cheri.

"Thought you were going to sleep all day," Renee said.

"Geneva up?" Cheri poured herself coffee. It smelled good. Better than when either she or Geneva made it—more like the way Auntie Marie's coffee smelled. Cheri added some cream and took a sip.

"Haven't seen her," Renee said, hoisting the baby over her shoulder for a burping. Cheri walked toward the hall, Geneva's room.

She tapped on Geneva's door but there was no response. In the pocket of her sweatshirt, she felt for the small wrapped gift—a ring for Geneva. She would let Geneva know that she was safe and that Cheri would say whatever she wanted her to say. She would protect Geneva from harm. They would be together.

Cheri turned the handle and pushed the door open. Her heart lurched forward in eagerness to give Geneva the present. She had waited so long.

CLINT HAD NOT ASKED Geneva to marry him at Christmas as she'd expected and now she was pregnant and waiting. He told her to get rid of it. Told her he was too young to settle down. He said he would never marry her. But Geneva still believed he'd come around. "If he doesn't marry me, I'll raise the kid myself," she told Cheri on the eve of their high school graduation. They were sitting on Geneva's bed, side by side, with their backs against the wall, drinking beer by candlelight. They could hear Auntie Marie's snores as she napped in her chair before the television. Cheri held Geneva's hand and handed her tissues when she needed to blow her nose from the crying.

"You could, you know," Cheri said. "I'd help you."

"You'd do that?" Geneva turned to her, looked at her.

"Of course," Cheri said. Back in her room she had a present for Geneva. Her plan was to give it to her after graduation the next day. It was a ring—a Claddagh.

GENEVA WAS NOT IN HER BED. Cheri ducked her head back into the hall—bathroom door was open, light off. Empty. She looked back down toward the kitchen. "She in the store?" she asked Renee.

"I haven't seen her," Renee said. "Not since the sheriff was here."

Cheri walked back through to the store. Empty. Lights off. Closed sign on. She went back to Geneva's room. Looked in the closet, under the bed. Geneva was not there, but there was an envelope on her pillow, addressed to Cheri.

The envelope contained a terse note and a lump of money—close to $2,000 in cash, in hundreds and some twenties. The note said that Geneva was gone. That she did not know when she would return. If ever.

Blackness tugged through Cheri's torso, pulling her from this world into some other, empty one where she was alone. When all the others had left her, Geneva had always been there, waiting for Cheri, waiting for her return, never leaving, never wavering. Even when she'd gone and married Clint, Cheri knew the two of them would be back together again, living as sisters did, loving each other. And now Cheri had driven Geneva away, sent her running for her life. She would wait for her return and if Geneva ended up in jail, Cheri would visit her every day or she would implicate herself so that they would be in jail together, passing notes through the bars, sending signals via hand mirrors. She would wait.

It was graduation day and they sat side by side on the stage of the hot auditorium. Normally, sitting there and waiting for the presentations to be over would have annoyed Cheri, but today was the day of days. Beneath their red robes, Geneva wore a white dress she had made and Cheri wore a pair of cut off shorts and a tank top. Auntie Marie had been horrified, but Cheri was unmoved. "What are they going to do? Not let me graduate?"

That morning, Geneva had gotten her period and even though she and Clint weren't talking, she had called and left Clint a message: You are off the hook.

Cheri decided to hold off on the ring, to wait until after the ceremony and all of the parties. She would bring Geneva someplace special in the moonlight—perhaps their spot in the woods, or the quarry. There she would make her presentation.

When all of the diplomas had been handed out and the well

wishers made their way toward the exits, Cheri lost sight of Geneva. She pushed through the crowds and out onto the stoop and there across the circular driveway, beneath the flagpole, was Clint on one knee before Geneva, pulling a ring out of his pocket, presenting it. Geneva hesitated, her response hanging back as the crowd held its breath. Cheri was about to move forward, call out to Geneva, "Don't do it. Don't say yes," when Geneva nodded and clapped her hands together and then apart, letting Clint slip the ring on her finger, letting him lift her up off her feet into the air.

The crowds of people clapped and cheered. Cheri stood silent. Soon Auntie Marie was beside her. "Isn't that something?" she said. "I never figured her for the marrying sort."

"Me neither," said Cheri. Back at home she hid the Claddagh ring in the back of her underwear drawer. She would leave this place. She would leave Auntie Marie. She would leave Geneva. And she would never come back.

14

THIS WAS THE PLACE where Geneva was meant to come. This was her pilgrimage. And those were the words that had come to her a few days before when she lay on the icy ground. The words were: *Leave here. Go find the answer. Go hear my voice. Listen for your calling. Find your guidance.*

On her way down the road, before a trucker had picked her up, she had remembered the flyer from the bus—the pilgrimage those people had been on. There was a church group in Plattsburgh that chartered this bus and after finding the church and reading their bulletin board, she saw that soon they would leave again. She would go with them.

She found a vacant hotel room on Lake Champlain and holed up for a few days, making phone calls, securing travel arrangements. Watching wind and snow blow across the nearly frozen water. She heard on the television that the investigation involving Rick and Plunker was closed. The local and federal authorities were satisfied that Plunker was the guilty party. It was done. She was free to go as she pleased. From Plattsburgh, she would take the church bus to St. Joseph's Oratory in Montreal. A bus of pilgrims as she'd seen. Surely no one would find her suspicious on such a trip, disfigured as she was. Ones such as her were always looking for hope, searching for answers. From Montreal she could slip away to anywhere, become anyone. It would be an easy trip. A quick trip. At the border she would list her reason for traveling as making a pilgrimage. A visit to St. Joseph's Oratory. She was a pilgrim. Simple, clean, plain, searching, searching.

On the day of her departure, she wanted to sleep as she waited on a hard pew in a nearly empty church for the bus. She wanted to erase from her mind all of the past, but found it on continuous loop instead. She kept coming back to Clint, how he had taken her to the prom. She had not expected it—that a boy like him, popular, handsome, would choose her. She was the prettiest girl in the class but she was parentless, poor. Some boys thought she might be easy in her vulnerability but ended up labeling her frigid instead when their advances were denied. Still, Clint had been sweet, unsure of himself, nervous, even, when he asked her, and he seemed genuinely pleased when she said yes.

Auntie Marie helped her make the dress—pale yellow against Geneva's dark skin. She seemed to glow when she put on the dress, they all said. Cheri sat on her bed, watching as she prepared for the night out, brushed her hair, applied lip gloss. No one had asked Cheri. Geneva had offered her to come along with her and Clint but Cheri had turned her down. "Proms are for losers," she said. Geneva wasn't bothered by this comment. She knew Cheri well enough to know when she was protecting herself.

Clint had told Geneva that the boys were scared of Cheri—her hair, her makeup, the outfits she wore. None of it was normal. "They think she's a dyke," he told Geneva. Geneva had defended Cheri against this charge but she couldn't be sure. "Anyway," he said. "She's not the kind of girl you bring to the prom." Geneva hadn't known that she herself was that kind of girl. Up until then she had counted herself equal with Cheri—equally reviled, equally ready to make a break for the outside world. This had been their plan. They would move away together. Take flight.

Auntie Marie had taken photos of Geneva and Clint, with Cheri hanging miserably in the background. She remembered the set of Cheri's face, how there had been some recognition there that things were now changing and would never be the same again. How there had been something about grief—the loss of their youth, that they weren't really sisters after all, that Geneva would never be hers alone again. Not ever.

WHEN THE TIME CAME, Geneva boarded the bus to Montreal. On it were many old ladies, tourists, small families. She stuffed her duffel bag at her feet and settled into her window seat, hoping that no one would sit next to her and ask questions. She thought she was safe, too, as by the time the driver settled in and prepared to shut the doors, her adjoining seat was still empty, but then an old lady lumbered on and took the seat, squishing her fat body up against Geneva's.

"First time?" the woman asked or said; which was unclear. She held a bulging plastic bag against her large belly, clasped fingers like sausage links.

Geneva nodded.

"I go every year for ten years," the woman said. "Wouldn't miss it. The only thing that will keep me from it is when I'm too old to travel. Even then I might make one of my grandkids push my wheelchair."

"Hmmm," Geneva murmured back.

Geneva turned her face back to the window in hopes that the

woman would shut up. The old woman reclined her seat and yawned. Thank God. Geneva tucked her body into the nook by the window, hoping that the old lady's skin would unclamp itself from hers. "What's that phrase? No matter where you go, there you are? I think it's something like that," the woman said. Geneva glimpsed to her side and saw that the lady had closed her eyes.

THEY ARRIVED IN MONTREAL as the sun was setting, early in the winter sky. "We've made it," her seatmate said, and thrust a hand in Geneva's direction for a shake. "Good luck," she said. "Peace be with you."

"Thank you," Geneva said. She watched the woman struggle out of her seat and join those already in the aisle, filing out of the bus. Geneva let people go by her and was the last to disembark. She wasn't sure what she should do. Where to go and what to say. She hadn't really planned on entering. She didn't feel worthy.

Women were moving toward the steps, leading up to the grand building. Others murmuring softly with their faces lifted to the sky.

The steps. Those would be the same Auntie Marie's father had knelt on and prayed for his miracle. She left the bus and followed the pack of women. Snow fell through the pink light of sunset. Geneva climbed a few steps before she sat down, not registering the cold. Cold was good. Like pain. She thought of her arm. Gone now. Gone. She thought of Plunker alone and dying on her behalf. It was a selfless act, she felt. He had been heroic and she resented it. He didn't have to save her. Not the first time and certainly not this second time. She hadn't asked for it. Not from any of them, not from Marie, not from Cheri.

And here among these people murmuring and chanting, she was alone. Perhaps she would stay here and join a convent. Spend her days in silence, flagellating or churning butter or making yogurt or whatever it was the nuns did. Being a nun would be easy for her. She would devote her life as a servant, a wife, to Jesus. She would be married to him even though he was long dead. She would love him easily and fully as she loved her dead auntie, as she loved her dead arm. She had been a nun for Auntie Marie all of these months since her death, after all. Devoting herself to Jesus wouldn't be so hard. She would be his perfect bride.

As the sun dipped lower in the sky, Geneva lost perception of how long she had been sitting. She had not eaten or drank anything since the previous evening and even then she hadn't had much. Her head felt light and free. She knelt, placed her palm on the stone before her and leaned her body forward until her head was on her hand.

She thought of the dead man. He was dressed in a white robe and hovering in the sky above her. He held out his hands and showed her his bare feet. There she saw the wounds of the martyr. His bleeding stigmata. And Marie was at his left hand and Plunker his right. All of them pure and clean. She had come to them in her dirty black clothes, reeking of sweat and blood. Not her blood. Blood. She fell down before them. With a basin of cool, clear water she bathed their feet, one by one and asked for forgiveness. It was the only way.

BEFORE SHE WAS SENT to the convent, Marie longed for her life to not be this simple one with her parents, where her days were filled with going to school and working the store. She longed for something grander. Something miraculous. Oh, to be a mystic like Saint Gertrude!

And when nothing did happen, despite all her prayer and want, she lied.

"I have had a vision," she told her mother. "A visitation." She spoke of a great light and sense of joy surrounding her. She spoke of the hands of Jesus coming forth and lifting her up. She spoke of how the light was passed to her, pressed within her. "I carry the light now," she said. "I carry it within me and I want to answer the call."

"It is a special gift," her mother said, humbled. And so Marie was sent away, behind the walls within which her simple mother was raised. It was because of this lie that her life shrank down to the size of a freckle and she, along with her hopes and desires, was broken down to nothing.

The lie was Marie's greatest sin and because of it she was not worthy of God and not worthy of Jesus and not worthy of a child of her own. It was because of the lie that she eventually left the convent and punished herself by going back home to live with her father, the beast. It was because of the lie she believed Geneva left her only to return again broken and unwhole. It was because of the lie that cancer consumed her. It was because of the lie that she let it.

GENEVA WOKE UP on the bus, reclined slightly in a seat. The woman who had ridden beside her was dabbing at her face with a damp cloth. "You fainted," she said when Geneva opened her eyes. "You were speaking," the woman said, and then whispered, "almost in tongues. It's the sign of a true believer." Geneva shut her eyes, seeking comfort in the darkness. "Ten years coming here," the woman said, "and I've not yet fainted. Maybe someday." Geneva closed her eyes again and slept.

When she woke the woman was gone. Possibly it had all been a dream or illusion. The bus was parked at a station. Harsh light from the street lamps cut through the dirty windows.

The bus driver was standing next to her seat. "This is the last stop," he said. Geneva didn't move. Where would she go? "Please," he said. "I'm off duty."

Reluctantly she left the bus and entered the station. People dozed on benches. Others bustled around pulling bags on wheels. At the ticket counter, Geneva asked the clerk where she could go from there. "How far do you want to go?" the clerk said.

"How far will $500 get me?" The clerk tapped into his computer and printed out a ticket. Vancouver, it said. All the way there. Yes. She would cross this country and she would find out how it was to live with such longing.

15

At first it was not such a problem, this stripping off the calendar months—December became January and a new year. January became February and a hope of spring. But then as February edged toward March and the fields across the way turned from hard ruts to soft mud, and snow and ice dripped down from the trees, Renee thought of the quarry deep in the woods. How the ice would soon melt away and Rick's body would be retrieved. She had never called his mother. Never let anyone back there in Florida know of his fate. Let them all think what she would have thought had he disappeared on her, which he eventually would have—that he had finally slipped full force into the lifestyle he had been toying with for years.

Still, visions of his body emerging from below the ice—pale and possibly kept intact by the cold, or worse, gnawed on by fish and whatever other creatures lurked at the bottom of the quarry—filled her with anguish.

Along with these thoughts of Rick, all of the complications and irritations of running the store weighed on her. The bills were constant and the sales scant. She had no idea how she and Cheri were going to keep this business going, but it seemed as though they would both die trying. A thought which depressed her. She didn't want to die there, running the store.

Now Titty's, she would have died there. There was simplicity to the life she'd left behind there. It was easy and often fun. Like Bike Week.

In some ways, things had turned out better than she could have hoped—she had her baby to take care of and Cheri seemed to be warming to her. Still, Renee couldn't deny that she felt a secret tension whenever she heard a Harley drive by. She felt an urge to flee so strong at times that she was amazed when she looked down and saw her two feet were still in the same place she'd left them.

When she could hold back her feelings not one minute longer, she called Titty's. It was early on a Saturday afternoon—before she was due to switch shifts with Cheri. She called and when someone answered the phone and in the background she heard the whoop and holler of Bike Week, she felt she might split down the middle with desire. To be there in the darkness of the bar on a hot afternoon, the light from outside flooding a long tube of floor each time a new customer entered. The dust and the smoke and the smell of gasoline and sweat and sex and beer. She wanted it all back. All of it.

But then Cree, awake from her nap, cried out in need from the back bedroom and Renee hung up the phone. For now she would stay put and take care of those who needed her. For now she was home.

Her meals with Cheri were joyless but for Cree, who was always banging the tray of her high chair and laughing and making noises. Renee told herself to be happy for this time with Cheri and not to push it. Not to force the girl to feel more for her than she was capable. Still, it would have been nice to have a friend if nothing more. Someone she could share her fears with about Cree. A few folks had asked questions and Renee had done well at keeping them quiet, but if anyone down in Florida ever came looking for the baby she wasn't sure what she would do. The fear was sometimes all encompassing, closing over her like the door of a casket, but then she would let her optimistic side take over and believe that it would all turn out for the best. She had, after all, saved the child's life. That had to count for something. Didn't it?

Often Renee stopped herself from saying how much the baby reminded her of Cheri when she was young. But once it did slip out. Renee slapped a hand over her mouth as soon as she said it.

Cheri threw her fork down on the table and crossed her arms over her chest. No sooner had she done that than she stood up and threw her hands in the air. "Are you kidding me? Are you even serious?" Cree's face crumpled and she sucked in breath as she watched Cheri. Renee went to the baby and picked her up from the high chair, shielding her face and shushing her.

"Oh, that's just perfect," Cheri said. "Of course, you'll protect your perfect little angel baby. But what did you ever do for me? I'm surprised you even remember that you gave birth to me, let alone remember what I was like as a baby."

"Cheri," Renee said, reaching for her, "I'm your mother."

"Auntie Marie was my mother," Cheri said, "You're just the whore who gave birth to me." Then she left them, Renee and Cree crying together in the kitchen.

"This is our home," Renee said to Cree. "We're going to make the best of it."

GENEVA AND CLINT WERE TO BE WED in early August, when the nights were cooler and the days yet warm. It would be a small to-do—just family mostly, of which Geneva had only Marie and Cheri. The night before the wedding she asked Cheri to join her at the fire pit. "Let's have a party," she said. "Just us."

"Okay," Cheri said, without enthusiasm. She'd been this way since the engagement. Geneva figured it was jealousy—maybe she wanted Clint herself? Maybe she wanted to be the one getting married? Maybe.

The day had been drizzly and gray, but the clouds disappeared that night as high pressure pushed a cold front through. Soon there would be frost and leaves changing color from their tips inward. Geese were already honking their way south and ferns burning at their edges were curling inward.

Fall came early to the north country. Geneva spent the nights between graduation and the eve of her wedding fantasizing how it would be to have her own house and family. She would want holidays to be special—Thanksgiving, Christmas. And they would have many children. She would love them all and above all else they would cherish their mother. Her life was just now beginning and though she knew there would be hard times, she firmly believed she and Clint would get through it all. They would be partners in this life. She wanted Cheri to be happy for her.

In a backpack, Geneva brought a six pack, a bag of chips, some cigarettes, and a bottle of champagne she'd bought at the liquor store. She'd never tasted it before and didn't think Cheri had either— but this was a night for celebration, a night of endings and new beginnings.

At the pit, Cheri set to work on building the fire. "You're awful quiet," Geneva said, sitting down on a log and pulling the backpack between her legs. She opened and emptied it as she waited for a word from Cheri.

"He's a pig," Cheri said.

"What?"

"Nothing," Cheri said. "Pretend I didn't say anything."

"Tell me what you're talking about," Geneva said. This was not good. It was Clint, Cheri meant. He was the pig.

Cheri cracked a branch in two with her foot, throwing it on top of the pile already waiting.

"Clint loves me, Cheri," Geneva said. "He's going to take care of me, give me a home." She watched as Cheri knelt down and built the fire, lit it, and poked until it was going strong. "Why can't you be happy for me?"

Cheri sat across the flames from her. They met eyes. There it was—that look. There it was. It was the one she'd come to know from men and boys but she hadn't expected it from Cheri, her friend, so nearly kin to her. She felt a sickening moment of revulsion, of distaste, but also she felt a flicker of love. She loved Cheri, her sister. Cheri looked away.

"If you marry him, I'm going away and never coming back," Cheri said. In her hand she held a stick with which she stabbed the ground again and again. Geneva saw that she was crying.

"You can't leave," she said.

"I mean it," Cheri said and wiped her face on her sleeve.

Geneva went to her, squatted next to where Cheri sat, touched her shoulder. "Please Cheri," she said. "Please don't go."

"Don't marry him," Cheri said, looking now at Geneva, daring her.

"I have to," Geneva said.

Cheri took Geneva's face in her hands then and kissed her, lips on lips. She kissed her and Geneva felt pity and horror growing, flying, like an enormous black bird in her chest. With wings and arms she pushed Cheri away. "Don't," she said.

Cheri got up and ran away into the woods and the night. Geneva called after her but her calls went unanswered. She sat by the dying fire and uncorked the champagne as the man at the store had taught her to. She drank straight from the bottle. It was not the joyful beverage she expected—instead her mouth was filled with bitterness.

She would not see Cheri again until the ceremony the next day, when Cheri stood up beside her and watched as she married Clint. Soon afterwards Cheri was gone from Marie's and from town all together. Gone forever, Geneva thought, never to return, never to forgive, never to be forgiven.

THIS COUNTRY NORTH of her had always been there and yet she'd never thought what it offered her. Space. Anonymity.

When she arrived in Vancouver, Geneva took a room in a boarding house and waited for further instruction. One night on the television in the main room, she saw an advertisement for the aquarium. The Beluga—white, fleshy, sleek. There was something about the way their bodies moved through the water. The pale flesh beneath the murk was so like the body of a man beneath ice. Then she knew what she must do.

She took a ferry to Vancouver Island. The trip was long in miles but seemed to pass quickly as Geneva drifted in and out of sleep— an ever present vision with her: one of water and her body floating, drifting out to sea. Once on land she took a bus across the island until she made it to Pacific Rim National Park and Tofino, a tiny fishing village. It could not have been more different than home and yet more similar. The people had their jobs to do. They had money to make in certain seasons. They had priorities. Tourists only stayed so long and after that there was still a house to heat, babies to feed.

She found a room at an inn and set out in the dying light of day to explore the village. The fishing boats in the marina were brightly colored—primaries of red and blue and yellow. Some offered tours, one of which she signed up for. They would be led to different bays and beaches from which they could more closely observe the majestic shoreline—the towering trees, the hills and mountains. Possibly they would see whales, orca.

There was only one other couple on the boat with her—older, British, enjoying a second honeymoon, perhaps. Geneva sat across from them and avoided eye contact. She didn't want to chat and even when they tried to engage her in conversation, she pretended not to understand English. They tried several other languages—French, German—before finally giving up on her and leaving her in peace.

The day was bright yet with high clouds and diamonds of light reflecting off the sea. She was glad she'd bought sunglasses earlier in the day and that she'd worn a scarf on her head to keep her hair from whipping into her face. The boat started with a lurch and as they left the mooring the tour guide began his routine. He was frustrated with the lack of understanding in Geneva's eyes, and focused exclusively on the couple. She listened to him with half an ear, but mostly she already knew what she had come for.

The boat edged along the coast and Geneva gazed out across the Pacific, wondering what was happening back home on such a day. Would the snow be melted? The ice? It was likely that, yes, the ice would be soft enough now that the authorities would have been able to pull the dead man from the deep waters of the quarry. And if not, she remembered that their plan had been to pump the thing later in the spring, fill in whatever cracks fed it, and leave it dry, a grave no more.

They would find his corpse on the bottom among the twisted debris—old cars, refrigerators. He would be pale, shriveled, a juicy grub—the meat falling easily from the bone. And he would still be dead because no amount of her wishing things had happened differently would change that. She had killed him. He was dead and not to be resurrected.

She looked over the edge of the boat and caught a glimpse of a school of fish as they darted by. Startled by their flashing scales, she sat back with a hand on her chest. The guide stopped talking and he and the old couple looked at her. She smiled to show she was okay, indicated with a wave of her hand that they should carry on.

It was a Saturday in March, when spring was possible but not yet in evidence. Still, the sun was stronger than it had been in months and the icicles hanging from the eaves above the store window dripped rhythmically, sploshing the hard ground. Four o'clock was nearing, which meant it was almost time to switch shifts with her mother.

Slowly through the days of short light and the nights of long darkness, Cheri and Renee had found a way that they could tolerate being in a room together: Cheri had learned to forgive just a little and Renee had learned not to expect too much. Life here in this horrible, desolate place was becoming possible again. At least, she believed, she could stay here until Geneva returned. Even if that meant waiting forever. She would.

The cruise had begun in early afternoon when the sun had long past peaked and was inching down the sky toward the horizon, but there was still much to see. Before long they made it into a cove surrounded by mountains and sky. Each break in the trees an eye staring at her, knowing. This was the place, but they were not alone. There were other boats around them, sailboats, motorboats, and other identical fishing boats. Geneva waited and watched as the boats thinned out, moved on back to the harbor or the next viewing point.

The guide said he had something important to show his passengers. With open arms, he directed them to the front of the boat, but Geneva hung back. He had promised them sea life—whales, dolphins. She watched as the guide pointed off into the distance. There was something about the way the water met the sky—the continuous line of it. Where did one begin and the other end? The older couple was engrossed in what he told them and no one noticed as Geneva slipped herself over the edge of the boat, letting herself dangle by her knees, until she could touch water with her fingers.

The water was colder than she expected and though her legs and good arm were strong, it was difficult for her to keep her head above the surface. She did not cry out. This was the place she was meant to be. Here was the core of all longing and understanding. She kicked off with her feet and floated on her back farther and farther from the boat toward the tree-lined shore. Soon they would no longer be able to see her if they cared to look. Soon she would be gone entirely.

Above were the blue sky and the clouds and the gulls circling, ever circling. In her ears the sounds of her breathing and the pressure of the surf. The sun flashed brightly from behind the clouds and she lost vision briefly, her sunglasses having been flung off her head when she tipped off the boat.

It was time, and though for an instant she felt panic followed by a strong will to live—so strong in fact that she almost turned over and called out—she did not stop paddling even as her body weakened.

Soon her good arm gave way, tensed up in the muscle, and she was left only her legs and feet, her shoulders and her neck. She kept on. She closed her eyes from the glare of the sun and let herself fall into the rhythm of her breath. This was what it would have been like in the womb, sightless and without fear.

It was time to let go then, to stop kicking and sink under. She allowed herself one more good breath and then she let go. She did not open her eyes, but sank, long hair stringing out around her, lifting up to the light above.

Lifting up by her hair.

That is where the hands of the woman caught her. Two surprisingly strong hands gripping her long hair and pulling her up and out into the bright light and the sounds of the gulls calling above them. Her first scent was that of the boat's gasoline, and her first vision, the trees and the eyes and the shore falling away as the woman expertly swam her in the lifesaving hold until they reached the boat. There the guide and the other man yanked her by her arm and the collar of her shirt until she was on board.

"You could have died," the woman said.

They wrapped her in tattered blankets and the woman and man rubbed her hand and feet until they turned from blue to pink. They did not say anything to each other as the boat headed back to port. Instead, Geneva looked back, away from the setting sun and toward the mountains, and out of trees flew dozens of creatures—bats or birds, she wasn't sure which—heading away from the comfort of darkness into the bleeding night, in search of sustenance and life.

Book Club
Discussion Questions

Early in the story, Geneva loses her arm. Does this loss seem to make her weaker or stronger? What does it symbolize?

To what does the book's title refer and how is it represented in the quest of each of the characters?

Sisterhood is important throughout the novel. Geneva and Cheri were raised like sisters. Is their relationship sister-like? Renee and Marie were half-sisters. Did their relationship seem sister-like?

What does Cheri's response to her feelings of rejection from Geneva say about her character? What does Geneva's response to Cheri's declaration of love say about her character?

How has her fear of abandonment affected Geneva's life and the decisions she makes?

In what way was the physical landscape important to each of the characters? What do we learn about the social, cultural, and religious make up of the town where Cheri and Geneva grew up?

What role does Iris play in the narrative? How do you characterize the relationship between her and Plunker?

Geneva kills Rick and uses Plunker to help her do so. Are they equally guilty of the crime? Why? Why not?

Plunker kills himself out of a sense of guilt and grief. Does Geneva similarly punish herself? If so, how?

Should Geneva be punished by the legal system? Why? Why not?

Did Rick deserve to die for his crimes? Why? Why not?

Time and again the characters come back to the abandoned quarry. What does it symbolize to each of them? In the same way, water is repeated throughout the novel, ending with Geneva in the ocean. Why is water so important symbolically?

In many ways, the characters repeat the mistakes of their past or continue on a destructive pattern. In what ways do they break free and break the cycle?

When Geneva leaves home, she goes on a pilgrimage. Why and what does she find there? Why does religion play such an important role within the book?

Renee takes in stray animals and loves babies and destructive men. What does this say about her personality? Does Cheri's personality in any way resemble her mother's personality? If yes, in what way? If no, why not?

Even though she dies early on, Auntie Marie remains a presence throughout the book. In what way does her original "sin" change the course of all of their lives?

Each of the characters carries a deep fear. What are those fears and how are they manifested?

What does Canada represent to Geneva? What other borders and boundaries are represented within the narrative?

In the end, we don't know whether Geneva and Cheri will ever see each other again. Do you think they will? Do you want them to?

What does the future hold for Cheri and Renee? Will they continue to grow their bond as mother and daughter? Do you want them to?

An Interview with Myfanwy Collins

Author Katrina Denza talks with Myfanwy Collins about
Echolocation, *her writing life, and the future.*

**Katrina: Do you remember the moment or moments in which you
were certain you wanted writing to be your life's work?**

I remember writing and illustrating my first story when I was six. I
felt something indescribable as I wrote it and came to make sense of
what I wanted to say.

I wrote throughout my childhood and young adulthood. I wrote
in journals and diaries. I wrote stories. Writing was always on my
mind, but as a young person I did not allow myself to believe that I
would ever devote myself to writing.

It wasn't until I was a senior in college when the woman who
came to be my mentor asked me, "Have you ever thought of writing
a novel?" that something clicked in me. I had thought of it but didn't
think I was worthy of doing so. She tore down all of those walls
for me. It was right there in that moment when I said, "Yes. I have
thought of writing a novel," that I believed I could do it.

There have been many doubts since that day twenty years ago and plenty of ups and downs but I've always believed since then that what I wanted to with my life was write.

Katrina: Writing is a lonely endeavor, and most of the difficult labor goes on behind the scenes for years and years without notice or reward. What keeps you going?

Having a community of writer friends has definitely kept me going. Seeing my peers succeed and fail and succeed some more gives me hope. My own small successes have kept me going.

A big motivator has been when people, strangers, have reached out in generosity and told me they liked something I wrote or that something I wrote moved them.

Mostly, though, there is something inside me that says, "Keep going."

Katrina: I'm always interested to know how other writers approach the work. What is your typical writing day like? Do you write longhand or type? What tools or rituals are essential for you? What would your ideal writing day be like?

Such an interesting question. I'm having a difficult time coming up with a response because my typical day is ever changing since becoming a mother.

I have never been a write-every-day person. Well, actually, if I'm working on a particular project I will try to write every day, but otherwise I don't sit down to write. Now, especially, I don't because I don't have time.

I remember the workshop at Tin House you and I were in,

Katrina. Dorothy Allison was our workshop leader and she spoke on the last day about the person who has the most difficult time writing is the mother with a child under age five. At the time, you were that person and while I sat beside you and wept with you and felt like I understood that it must be very difficult, I had no idea how difficult it was for you. I do now.

I'm in writing survival mode now. I write when I can or when I am especially compelled. My son starts kindergarten next year and I don't know what I'll be doing in terms of work or school, but I'm hoping to have just a little bit more time for writing then, but I just don't know.

As for tools, I mostly use my computer. I started out writing stories when the only option was longhand and typewriter and, frankly, no matter how people want to romanticize it, I found it to be a pain in the ass. I type really quickly, but I make errors, and I love to be able to cut and paste. When I got my first word processor (I think I was a junior in college), I felt like a rainbow ended on top of my desk and planted the pot o' gold there.

I do still keep a journal and write longhand in it, but I don't do my creative writing that way. The plain fact is my handwriting is illegible and I can type like a maniac.

Katrina: To whom do you write? Do you have a certain reader in mind, and if so, does that reader remain the same or does he or she change with each new project?

I honestly don't have a reader in mind. I suppose I should have a better answer than that but I don't. I guess I don't go so far as to think about the reader as I write. I'm just in the moment and going with what comes to me. If I felt the need to write for a particular reader, I think I would not be able to write. I would be thinking too much (if that makes sense).

Katrina: Tell us about your revision techniques. Do they differ depending on the size of the project?

I love revision. I find it such a relief. Okay, I'm saying this as I stare down the barrel of a major project for which I must get words on a page. So I'm seeing revision as the Holy Grail right now. When I'm revising, I yearn for the fresh project and putting words on the page.

Honestly, I really do like revision. Or, at least, I don't hate it.

As for my process, for things like short stories and flash fiction, I tend to workshop and get feedback from other writers. I can revise a story for months or years. I typically revise right in the document and save new versions. When I'm nearing the end, I print out and revise on paper.

I have friends, trusted readers (like you, Katrina), who have been invaluable to my process, as I can always count on them to give me useful feedback.

For novels, I tend to not let anyone see the manuscript until I have at least a first draft (though usually not until I have a second or third draft). I have tried to do it piecemeal and sometimes that really works but sometimes it leaves me feeling like I can't move forward.

I began writing *Echolocation* as individual stories with the intention of it being a novel-in-stories. I workshopped each of those stories individually. After five or six stories, I gave up on that process and just started writing chapters and keeping them mostly to myself.

I finished the first draft a couple of weeks before I gave birth. I then sent the manuscript to my agent and gave into my contractions. I revised the manuscript a few months later with her notes. Since then it's gone through several other major revisions.

Katrina: You're a busy woman. You have a family; you've been an editor for a major journal; you're now working on your Master's degree. What advice would you offer someone who's struggling to find time to write?

The biggest thing for me is to get out of my own head and to stop listening to the voices that say, "You can't do this," or, "You don't have time to do that." If it is truly worth it to you to accomplish something, you will make the time.

When I went back to school, I didn't know how I was going to have time to do it and everything else. Here I sit having finished my final class with my thesis partially written and I realize that once I stopped telling myself that I couldn't do it and that there wasn't time, I did it. I got it done.

Also, setting my own internal priorities has helped. I've been overwhelmed the past few months with everything I have to do. Of course, everything to do with my son comes first. As for my work, I try to prioritize what is necessary to do that particular day by keeping a running list in my head. For instance, right now, my kitchen is a mess and I need to start reading *The Limits of Interpretation* by Umberto Eco for the next chapter of my thesis. I should probably vacuum. I have several emails to respond to and phone calls to make. But this interview is what I have in my mind as necessary to work on right now.

Of course, I am also fortunate to have a tremendously supportive partner in my husband. He always works to help find time for me to get my work done, but even then it's all about me shutting out those negative voices. We are truly our own worst enemies, sometimes.

Katrina: Much is made, in a writer's development, of the concept of voice. You have a distinct voice and as long as I've known you it's always been there. I can pick any Myfanwy Collins story, or novel, or flash fiction and be able to definitively identify it as such even if your name isn't attached. Can you tell us about voice? How did you come to yours? Did anyone try to steer you away from it?

Thank you for the compliment. What a great question. My voice is not something I consciously worked on. With that said, I believe it has become stronger and more evident as I've worked on my craft as the two seem intertwined to me. Really, what I think has happened is that as I became more confident in my writing, I more readily listened to the voice that speaks within me.

I'm not sure I can explain this well, but it's not my own speaking voice; it is a voice I hear as I write fiction. I know that might not typically be the way one describes narrative voice but that's the best I can do to explain how it works for me.

Katrina: Your novel's opening scene is a punch to the gut and a brilliant way to begin a story. What was the inspiration for it?

It all started with Geneva. First she came to me and then I knew that something dramatic had to happen to her. The story of the chainsaw and the arm was a story that a nurse who worked in a rural hospital told me one time. The difference was that the victim in her story was a young man who had been cutting wood with his father. After the accident, his father told him to run because he knew the adrenaline would save him and that they had limited time.

It's been over twenty years since she told me that story and I kept it in my mind not sure I would ever use it. I just knew that it held a power over me and that it spoke about our will to survive.

Katrina: There's such a strong sense of place in *Echolocation*. I was raised in the next state over and so much of your novel's setting, the flora and fauna, the character of the people, resonated with me. Why did you choose that particular part of the country?

I grew up in the Adirondack Mountains, where the novel is set. My heart absolutely lives in that rugged, beautiful, dangerous, loving place. I find myself drawn back there again and again as a setting for my writing. There is something so dramatic about the landscape and about the remoteness. We were only an hour away from Montreal but it felt like a different world from the dairy farms, the abandoned mines, the woods.

I also have a great deal of affection for the people of the place—their toughness and their ability to survive in the sometimes harsh environment.

Katrina: Though flawed, your female characters are all incredibly fierce, even Renee, though she may not appear so at first glance. Was this a conscious choice? What were the challenges, if any, in working with so many strong characters?

They all appeal to me—the women, the men. There is something about each of the characters that I love; even the characters who do horrible things have some kernel of life inside of them that shows me their humanity, but the women, yes, especially I love them. I grew up in a world of female energy. My mother had six sisters. My father had four sisters. I have three sisters. Most of my cousins are female. Men do not intimidate me, but strong women do. But then I am strong and I know this about myself. I will not give up and I'm drawn to women who are like me. All of my female friends and family members are fierce in their own ways.

Katrina: *Echolocation* **contains complex story lines all woven seamlessly together. What's your secret? Did you outline or did you allow your intuition to guide you? Did you have any difficulties in tying everything together?**

Thank you. I'm so pleased you found it so. I have an ability to keep the nuances of a storyline in my head as I read or write. It helps when writing my own work or editing the work of others. I'm not sure where it came from. Perhaps from being so long a student of literature or maybe it came from the way my sisters and I used to play as child. We would create a world and keep the storyline going for days and sometimes weeks. Or, it could just be something I was born with. Regardless, that ability was immensely helpful in writing this novel.

The challenge came when I came to do my last major revision. At that point, Victoria Barrett, my brilliant editor at Engine Books, suggested a major change to the manuscript; she suggested a remove an entire story line. It was a real light-bulb-going-off moment for me because what she suggested was exactly what needed to happen to the book but I simply could not see that.

Once I completed that revision and had others read it, it came to light that I had introduced several errors in logic that needed to be addressed. The problem was that I had answered all of the open questions in my deleted storyline and so, in my mind, the questions were answered and I could not see the holes myself in the manuscript. This is one place (among many) where other readers are so valuable and that is in pointing out your errors in logic.

Katrina: I'm astounded by your ability to render character with precision and economy. All of your characters' voices are so different and yet all are held true to your authorial voice. How do you do it? Do you have any techniques or does this kind of thing come naturally to you?

Writing in the third person really helped me achieve a consistency of voice over all, while still allowing me to show each character as individual. The third person allows that over-arching, almost cinematic ability to give the entire piece the feel of oneness and yet still allow for the uniqueness of each character to shine through.

Katrina: Auntie Marie chose not to seek treatment for her cancer, believed actually that her health and her life were in God's hands, and the local people consider her a hero for it. Did you know anyone like this? What are your personal beliefs regarding her decision?

Yes, I did know someone like Auntie Marie. I knew a woman who did not seek treatment. I thought she was tremendously brave, but I ached for her for the pain she suffered. My personal beliefs are that adults should be allowed to do whatever they want to do with their own bodies so long as they are not physically harming another person. I believe adults should be allowed to choose how they want to die, so long as they are not putting others at risk (especially children).

Katrina: Auntie Marie spent her life trying to atone for a lie she told when she was young, a lie about a vision she'd received that set her apart from ordinary folk, and yet, as she nears the end, she never recognizes that she's already paid too high a price for such an innocuous sin. What does this say about religion and faith?

I grew up Catholic, though I am Catholic no more. With that said, I respect people of faith (unless they use their faith to hurt or belittle or exclude others). I have seen how people have used their faith to get them through difficult circumstances and I believe that is a good thing.

Marie believed her faith was her strength. When the truth was her strength fed her faith. She gave as much to it as it gave to her.

She did lie and she did punish herself for that lie, but I don't think that is anything different from what any of us do to ourselves on a daily basis. We are forever beating ourselves up for our perceived sins of not being smart enough, or more beautiful, or better at work than the guy in the cubicle next to us. I wish we would be kinder to ourselves. Maybe we need to daily read the Mary Oliver poem "Wild Geese" and commit it to memory until it is like a prayer, especially remembering those precious lines: "You only have to let the soft animal of your body love what it loves."

Katrina: In Native American animal medicine, the bat symbolizes, among other things, rebirth and the ability to see through illusion. How has Renee been reborn? What illusions does Cheri come to see through? Geneva?

Wow, that is really cool. I had no conscious idea of that connection. Renee has been reborn into motherhood. With Cree she is able to become the mother she should have been to Cheri and thereby model better behavior for her daughter. Cheri is reborn in forgiveness and love. She forgives Geneva for rejecting her and forgives herself for laying bare her emotions. She lets herself open up again, just a little bit, to love. Geneva experiences both a physical and a spiritual awakening. Her rebirth is a rite of passage and a vision quest and in that the bat comes into play as her guardian.

Katrina: Which character is your favorite? Your least favorite? Which character surprised you? Which one wouldn't cooperate?

In the first drafts of the novel there was a character named Hobbey whom I adored. His was the story line that Victoria suggested I cut and she was absolutely right to say so. Since I was so into him, I couldn't see that he didn't really fit in the story and that I kept squashing him into scenes and scenarios where he had no business being. His story is his own. And while he's gone from *Echolocation*, he's not gone entirely.

I have a great deal of affection for all of the characters—even those who do horrible things. With that said, I really feel for Plunker. He so wanted to be good and to have some beauty in his life.

Auntie Marie surprised me the most. I had thought she would continue to be saintly in my eyes and then I realized that she was human, which is good.

Katrina: Plunker was a particularly interesting character to me. I found it noteworthy that he was convinced that he loved "his woman" and yet failed to notice her deterioration right in front of his eyes. How did the character of Plunker show up to you? And I'm going to try to sneak this one in... is Geneva Iris's child?

I'm so glad you found him interesting. I really wanted him to be well rounded and not come off like a caricature. You can be uneducated and still have an inner life.

Plunker is an amalgamation of people I've encountered throughout my life. Part of him is also part of me. I wanted him to be this certain type of person you might see or be able to identify in the North Country and also I wanted him to have, as I said above, this identifiable inner life.

His woman is really all he has in his life and so he is unable to see that she is not there anymore. He sees her as he wants to see her. I understand this reaction so fully from watching beloved people and creatures fade away and/or die. The mind does not want to witness the weakness.

Ah ha. You caught on (of course!) to something I was trying to hint at but never made explicit. I was suggesting that Iris might have been Geneva's mother but I never fully went there because I wasn't sure in my own mind if she was. Perhaps I wasn't sure because Iris wouldn't have known anymore. Her lost children ceased to even exist to her as living beings. They had become spirits.

Katrina: One of the themes in *Echolocation* is loss. Mother loss, loss of home, loss of love. Some of these losses in the book cannot be regained, can never be, and your characters must come to accept this fact and most do. How has loss colored your life? Your writing?

There have been times in my life when I've focused too heavily on all that I've lost and now I'm in a place where I spend a great deal of my time focusing instead on what I have and expressing gratitude for it. But this does not take away from the fact that I have lost many people I love. My father when I was ten. My mother in my early 30s.

I have lost friends and family members. I have lost love. I write about loss a lot, I would say.

Our beloved dog died recently. This was the first time I've had to mourn openly with my son. I have lost people while my son has been alive but he didn't have a relationship with those people and so my mourning was private. Our dog was a part of our family and my son has known him since he was born. Of course, a child's grief is more matter-of-fact and less obviously lingering. As his mother, I could not openly wallow in my grief as I would have liked to do, but that was okay, too. There is always life and living to attend to.

In *Echolocation*, I move the characters pretty quickly past the grief stage of losing Marie. That choice was intentional. They are in survival mode. There is no time to wallow when you are trying to survive.

Katrina: Renee has, for most of her life, acted out of self-interest and yet near the end she takes a great risk to save a baby unrelated to her. Does she believe that by saving this baby, she's saving herself? Her daughter? Do you believe redemption is always possible?

I do believe that redemption is possible and that people can change. I've changed as I've grown and become wiser. I've become more patient with people as I've settled into motherhood. I don't believe one can erase all past wrongs by simply changing, though.

Renee won't let herself believe that she did anything wrong by leaving Cheri behind. She takes on the baby because she likes to adopt creatures and people whom she perceives as weaker than herself. She believes she can save them and change them and make them better. She is childlike and lives in the world of magical thinking. And yet she shows remarkable strength in her will to keep the baby safe. She believes she needs Marie to keep them safe and what she learns (though maybe never consciously accepts) is that she is strong enough to save them herself.

Katrina: One of the truths I found in *Echolocation* is that we are destined to repeat the cycles and challenges presented to those that came before us unless we can somehow break free. Though Cheri is as careless with her body as her mother was, she broke the cycle of mother loss. She does not get pregnant only to give the child to someone else to raise. What about Cheri enables her to be different?

I believe that Renee did, in a way, save Cheri by leaving her behind. Cheri was then allowed to learn more about how to become an adult from Auntie Marie and learn how to care about others from Geneva. She was still imprinted by her early years with her mother but was also wounded enough to know what she needed to do to keep herself safe. It is when she is in times of distress that she acts out again with her body. Her love for Geneva and witnessing Geneva's sacrifice is what gives her the strength to finally change and stay behind and wait. In doing so, she is given time to become a family with her mother and Cree.

Katrina: What insights regarding writing did you discover after finishing this book?

Be honest. Write from the dark part of your brain. Do not be afraid of what you're writing and if you are afraid, write it anyway.

Katrina: What's next?

I have a manuscript on my hard drive that needs a rewrite. It was initially written for a Young Adult audience but now I'm going to just write it as I want to write it because I've held back too much. It simply doesn't sing yet.

Once I finish my M.A., I am thinking about going on for an MFA in creative writing as I would really like to teach creative writing. I have a degree in education already and so have the chops for teaching, in general, it's just learning how to teach the craft that I need more schooling in.

Other than that, I have to go scrub some toilets. And fold some laundry. And clean my kitchen.

Katrina Denza's stories have been published in several literary journals, most recently Passages North, PANK, Gargoyle *and* REAL: Regarding Arts and Letters. *In 2011 she was awarded a Carol Houck Smith Contributor scholarship for the Bread Loaf Writers' Conference.*

Acknowledgments

I offer my humble gratitude to Victoria Barrett for bringing *Echolocation* into the world. Thank you, Victoria, for sharing your brilliant mind with me and for saying yes to this book. You are truly a force of nature and I am fortunate to spend time in your orbit. Thank you to Penn Whaling, agent extraordinaire, for sticking by me all of these years and for being one of the best readers I know. Penn, I thank you for your intelligence, your grace, and your persistence.

I hold you in the highest regard, Ann Blaisdell Tracy, my first writing mentor and my dear, dear friend. Thank you for the world you have given me. I extend a heartfelt thank you to Pat Hoffmann and John Shout, for believing in me and encouraging me when I was young and green.

I thank my departed parents, Bud and Lynn, for bringing me into this world and teaching me to love nature and books. I thank my dear sisters, Michaela and Catherine, for always being by my side no matter how far apart we are. I thank my sister Kim for caring for me when I was small. I thank my parents-in-law, Mary & Dick Dreghorn and Gordon Dean & Hedley Yost, for treating me with love as though I were their own child. I thank my sisters-in-law and brothers-in-law: Fab, Joy, Billy, Larry, Karin, Lyn, John and Steve (RIP). And I thank my nieces and nephews: Aaron, Ryan, Frances, Hailey & Andrew, Philip, Justin, Drew, Liam, Ainsely, Sacha, Michael, and Alec. Thank you also to my wonderful aunts, uncles, and cousins.

I would be lost without the friendship of: Caroline Ash, my best friend who has always believed in me even when I did not believe in myself; and Maryanne Dower, beloved friend and part of the family.

For their endorsement of this book and for their dear friendship, I thank: Ellen Meister, who is always so generous with her time and with her wisdom; and Pia Ehrhardt, who is a generous guide and an inspiration. I am also most grateful to: Katrina Denza and Kathy Fish, inspiring writers and generous friends. All four of you make me want to be the best writer and mother I can be.

From the bottom of my heart, I thank: Patricia Parkinson, Ellen Parker, Kelly Flanigan, Alicia Gifford, Kirsten Snipp, Jordan Rosenfeld, Stephanie Anagnoson, and Pam Mosher, who read this manuscript in whole or in part as it was coming together and who have helped me in innumerable ways on this journey.

For their unwavering friendship and belief in me over the years, I am grateful to: Anne Boyea, Kim Jiguere, Holly Chase, Jen Potter, Michael Powers & Angela Mellon, Jeff Resnick, Sue Blankenship, Joan Jolley, Louise Snow, John & Cheri Garrett, and Tommy Tucciarone. I thank those who have inspired me and/or shown me kindness along my writing path; I will never forget what you've done for me: Eric Spitznagel, Kim Chinquee, Randall Brown, Roxane Gay, Robin Slick, Maryanne Stahl, Susan DiPlacido, Beverly Jackson, Dave Clapper, Ray Collins, Don Capone, Jennifer & Adam Pieroni, Marcus Grimm, Bonnie Zobell, Alia Yunis, Matthew Quick & Alicia Bessette, Steve Owen & Rebekah Hall, Deena Drewis, Michael Croft, Tom Jenks, and Peter Grandbois.

For those writers who have generously given their time to read and endorse this book, I thank you: Dorothy Allison, Ron Currie, Laila Lalami, and Benjamin Percy.

Finally, I thank my beloved son and husband. Thank you for showing me where my heart is, Henry. And as for you, Allen... I know you did not want to be thanked here, but there are not enough words to thank you for all you've given me, which is everything. Love.

About the Author

MYFANWY COLLINS was born in Montreal, Canada, grew up in the Adirondack Mountains of New York State, and now lives on the North Shore of Massachusetts with her husband and son. Her work has been published in *The Kenyon Review*, *AGNI*, *Cream City Review*, *Quick Fiction*, and *Potomac Review*. A collection of her short fiction, *I Am Holding Your Hand*, is forthcoming from PANK Little Books in August 2012.

CPSIA information can be obtained at www.ICGtesting.com
Printed in the USA
LVOW110907020212

266455LV00001B/2/P

9 780983 547792